WHATEVER
TO
ROBIN BUTT

R.E. HAINES

Message from the Author

Hello dear friend, thank you for choosing to pick up my book and I hope you enjoy reading this simple story.

It is an exaggerated but humorous account of some of the memorable moments I had growing up.

Some of the events written are true, I'll let you decide which they are... Hopefully, you are a fan of caravan holidays like me, and I hope you will find something to make you laugh, smile, or even reflect on in this story. If you happen to be reading this while on holiday yourself, then I hope you will enjoy it even more! I am a working bus driver and not a professional author, so please go easy on my story if you think it can be a little amateur at times.

I sometimes laugh out loud to myself while thinking about many of the things written in this story while on my bus, the passengers probably think I'm mad, and what the heck I probably am. *R. E Haines*

Chapter 1

OLD SCHOOL

Robin appeared to be in a trance as he stared at the messy bookshelf in the cluttered headteacher's office. There were piles of files and boxes all over the place, and the desk was littered with pens, stacks of folders and screwed-up paperwork everywhere, it was a tip.

Mr Bourneview sat in his swivel chair waiting and wondering what had gripped Robin's attention so badly, before realising it was the large collection of books stored awkwardly on the bookshelf next to him. He interrupted Robin's distraction and went on to ask,

'Are you aware of the boys climbing onto the school roof outside school hours? They're causing me a right headache,'

'Yes, Mr Bellview, I mean sir. It's not me or Lucas doing it,' replied Robin as he garbled worriedly, now giving his full attention to the Headteacher.

'Robin, have you forgotten I'm Mr Bourneview, not Bellview.'

'Sorry Sir,' apologised Robin nervously.

'Well, all right. 'And of course, I know it's not you. You wouldn't do anything as stupid as that. You only need to stand on top of the vaulting horse in PE to get vertigo, am I right?

'Yes Mr Bourneview, but I'm getting better at not passing out.'

'Yes-yes of course.'

Mr Bourneview wiped his glasses with a tired old handkerchief.

'Now back to the issue in hand my boy. You see, I already have a rough idea of who's climbing the roof, but I need proof, some evidence before I take any action against them.' Robin's fingertips began to sweat, 'So, do you know who they could be? He asked nervously. 'I think so, but I couldn't get a close enough look and by the time they had gone Mr Moleshill threatened me.'

'What for?' asked Robin. Mr Bourneview looked out of the window and explained.

'He said if he catches me hiding in his Privet again, he will take off both my legs with his rusty hoe.'

'That's not very nice,' said Robin as he began to tremble. 'Are you alright boy!?' Asked Mr Bourneview when he saw Robin shudder.

Robin paused, He wondered if snitching on the boys would be wise, and remembered the day when those nasty bullies stole his lunch box, threw the contents all over the floor of the boys' toilets, and stamped on his strawberry, leaving behind the little teaspoon in a small puddle beneath the urinals. He wondered what kind of punishment Mr Bourneview had in mind. Then he remembered when David Thomas offered him a so-called sweet from a sandwich bag, only to find out after he'd eaten it that it was a used urinal block taken from the toilets.

Mr Bourneview still waiting patiently for Robin to respond. Robin looked up at the ceiling squeezing his eyes tight shut and began to reel the boy's names

off counting them off his fingers. "David Thomas, Mike Redford, and Tom Climber," he said.

Mr Bourneview peered over his glasses contently and leaned back into his swivel chair rubbing his hands together with a sense of accomplishment.

'I thought as much,' he said twiddling his thumbs.

Robin was relieved and satisfied he'd finally gotten his revenge.

'Now son, I have a question, how did you know it was them climbing the roof? Have you heard talk of them doing it?'

'No Sir, I've seen them for myself when I've been over the golf course.'

Now Robin was worried that there was a chance he would get in trouble for trespass.

'*Robin?*' Mr Bourneview said disappointedly.

Robin's face turned pale.

'And you didn't think to come and tell me?'

'Tell you that I've been trespassing?'

What? No man! not telling me that they've been up on my roof?

What were you doing over there anyway? Building camps? Treehouses?'

'No? Replied Robin.

'Well, I would if I were your age.'

9

'I go there to collect lost golf balls with Lucas and his dog.'

Mr Bourneview seemed intrigued.

'Is that a fact? And then what do you do when you've collected enough of them? You must have hundreds by now.'

Mr Bourneview adjusted his glasses a second time.

'We don't do anything with them, just collect them,' said Robin.

Mr Bourneview seemed puzzled but amused and scratched his beard.

'Well, I suggest you take them up to the driving range and have a jolly good blast with them,' tapping the arm of his chair.

'Ay, sir?' asked Robin, unsure of why he was not in trouble yet.

Mr Bourneview stood up and admired the framed poster of Sedgley golf course on the wall, with both hands held behind his back.

'Yes, what a splendid idea,' he said.

'Tell you what,' turning back to Robin, 'Bring them to me I'll show you how to smack those balls.'

Mr Bourneview snatched his cup of tea from his desk, spilling it clumsily everywhere in excitement.

Robin tried to keep a straight face and said, 'Or I could just take them back.'

'No boy! We'll take them to the playing field and give them a jolly good smack, bring Lucas along with you, they are his share after all. Do either of you have any clubs?'

Robin reached into his pocket which made Mr Bourneview laugh.

'What are you doing? He asked, 'I hope you don't keep them in there.'

'Why ever not?' wondered Robin pulling his hand back out covered in melted chocolate, Mr Bourne-view rubbed his chin. 'I will bring some which I have lying around in my garage, it would be good to blow the dust off them and the fresh air will do us all good too, we spend far too much time in these school walls wouldn't you agree? Robin?'

'Well, yes.'

'Good, now let's look at these books you were so keen to see. A little reward for dobbing those boys in ay?' Moving towards the bookshelf on his swivel chair, Mr Bourneview placed his hand on top and turned to Robin.

'Are there any of these books that take your interest'.

'Yes!' Robin pinched his bottom lip and peered over.

'I can't make out what they are from here though Sir.'

'Well, let's have a closer look, shall we?'

Mr Bourneview left his chair and knelt to get a closer look at the books. 'I have all sorts here, "Robinson Crusoe", "Time Machine", "Food for the Academic Mind".'

'Oh? How did that get in there?' he wondered as he pulled out The Demon Headmaster and added it to his already cluttered desk.

Mr Bourneview continued. 'The famous five".'

'Yes!' said Robin joyfully.

'Here, take it.'

Mr Bourneview handed the book over to Robin and sat back at his desk. He began rummaging through some overdue letters to be read he hadn't picked up yet.

'You can let yourself out and bring those golf balls into school tomorrow, I'll bring the clubs and we'll give those balls a good smack up the playing field. Meet me back here after school, will you?'

'Yes Sir,' replied Robin as he tried to open the door. The door handle came off in his hand.

'Okay Robin, I've got a lot of work to get through. And you need to get back to class. Enjoy the book

'Robin was panicking not knowing what to do holding the door handle.

Mr Bourneview turned around wondering why Robin hadn't left the room yet. 'Robin! Why can't you open that door?'

Robin showed the handle in his hand.

'Oh piddle-wink and poppycock! What have you done?'

'I'm sorry Sir' apologised a very distressed Robin.

Mr Bourneview got out of his chair, looked at the door, and took the handle from Robin's hand.

'*Robin,*' he said disappointedly, 'You do realise that I can't fix this, being an academic man. You seem a practical lad though, here, you try.'

He handed the handle back to Robin.

Robin tried to put the handle back on but pushed the Spindle through its shaft in the process, they heard it clatter on the corridor floor on the other side. They looked at each other and then back at the door, they began to bang it and shout for help.

'It's no good,' said Robin.

'No, it's not,' agreed Mr Bourneview, 'Nobody can hear us.'

'There's only one thing for it,' he suggested.

'What's that?' asked Robin.

'We'll have to smash the window.'

'What with?' asked Robin.

'Hang on,' said Mr Bourneview.

'To what? Why don't we just call the fire brigade?'

'No Robin! I'm already on a warning with them.'

Robin picked up the office chair and threw it to-wards the window, it bounced off the desk and fell to the floor bringing with it all the clutter.

'No man! Here's how you do it.' Mr Bourneview picked up the chair and flung it with all his might, and it smashed through the window with a blast.

Robin picked up the teacup from the desk and threw it forthwith.

The chair flew and hit Mrs Haynes's car which was parked outside putting a dent into the driver's door.

The teacup followed cracking her windscreen.

The police turned up along with the fire brigade.

A fire person, who was a man came bursting through the wood of the door and snatched Robin pulling him out of the office with one hand.

Mr Bourneview was found hiding under the desk by a police officer who was a lady.

'Here!' She asked, 'What's been going on in here then?'

Mr Bourneview was interviewed by the police and was now on a final warning with the school governors.

Later that day after school, Robin got changed and called for his best friend Lucas. He waited outside while Lucas got ready. As they walked down the road, Lucas suggested they go to the Cotwall End Valley nature reserve. Robin hesitated; he had always found it a spooky place and it gave him the creeps.

'Hey, Mr Bourneview said that we can use his golf clubs if we take our balls with us to school tomorrow and play with them on the playing field after school,' said Robin excitedly.

Lucas was shocked, 'What!?' he asked intuitively.

'Oh yeah, he said for us to take the balls we found from the golf course.'

'Hang on, why would you tell him we take golf balls from the golf course?' asked Lucas angrily.

'It was the only way I could tell him who'd been climbing the school roof,' said Robin defensively.

Lucas looked sternly at Robin and asked, 'And what if they find out that it was you who grassed on them?'

Robin wondered, 'How would they?' he asked.

Lucas shook his head and said, 'I suppose playing with our balls on the playing field doesn't sound like a bad idea; Okay, I'm up for that.'

'See, I thought you might,' said Robin.

'Are we going to meet him on the field?' asked Lucas.

'No, he said for us to call for him at his office, do we have to go to Cotwall End? I don't want to go over there; can't we find some balls instead?'

'You need to find some, there's nothing to be scared of over Cotwall End.'

'We'll there's talk of the grey lady,' said Robin.

'What! you don't believe that do you?'

Robin Trembled, 'No, but I wouldn't like to find out either,' he said.

'Yes, you do believe it, look at you; how are you gonna get a girlfriend thinking like that all the time, and being scared of everything?'

'I don't need one of those, what's that got to do with_'

'Shh!' interrupted Lucas, 'Do you hear that?' hitting Robin on the arm.

'No?' said Robin.

Lucas started to jump around flapping his arms and acting like a chicken, 'It's the flying headless chicken,' he said.

'I don't know who's worse, you or your dad, and if you make me jump like that again, I'm not going.'

'Oh, come on, don't be such a Jessy, and what do you mean you don't need one, everyone needs a girlfriend? And don't give me that, I've seen how you look at Kate.'

'I haven't looked at her like anything, and where's yours? since everyone needs one so badly.' Asked Robin.

'I'm working on it,' replied Lucas.

Robin and Lucas had reached the bottom of the estate, where Cotwall End Nature Reserve was opposite across the road. Lucas ran across Cotwall End Road and approached the entrance of Cotwall End Valley.

'Wait for me,' said Robin.

He ran as Lucas waited at the stile, Lucas put out his hand and said, 'Ladies first.'

'Shut up,' said Robin as he mounted the stile.

They entered the wood and walked the narrow shadowy path sheltered by trees. Eventually, they reached the stream at the bottom of the valley, they crossed it using a fallen tree and found a path on the other side. Robin and Lucas followed it for quite some time, with Robin occasionally looking over his shoulder.

Lucas stopped walking.

'Let's go this way,' he suggested.

'Why? There's no path that way,' said Robin.

'Oh, come on.'

'No! I've come this far, is that not enough?'

Lucas spotted a square hole in the ground; it was about a meter square with a four-inch timber frame.

'let's go down it,' said Lucas.

'No way! Said Robin as he peeked down into the dark void,

'There could be a ta- rantula down there.'

'I'm not even going to laugh at that one,' said Lucas,

'Don't be so stupid.'

'I'm not stupid! there could be a false widow, or?' –

'A grey lady,' interrupted Lucas.

'No! A body,' said Robin.

Lucas thought Robin may have a point and became concerned. 'Okay, we can go back for a torch, then come back.

Robin agreed just for an excuse to get out of there. They headed back to get a torch. It wasn't too long until they were back at Lucas's house. Lucas rummaged through his dad's garage. Lucas's dad Lennard came in, he must have heard Lucas going through everything. 'What are you looking for now?' he asked.

'We need a torch,' replied Lucas.

'What the heck for?'

'We found a_'

'Shut up Robin,' snapped Lucas.

Lennard seemed interested.

'Yes, found a what and where?' he asked.

'All right, near a tree by the river we found a hole in the ground, on the other side of the river in the woods,' explained Lucas.

'Oh no you don't, that place is riddled with old mine shafts, and what do you mean the other side of the river? There's no river in there, just a stream.'

'Oh Dad, we just want to shine a torch down the hole I found.'

Lennard rubbed his face and looked at the two of them.

'Right, I'll show you where there's one,' he said while pulling a box from the shelf on the wall, and singing, *"The Riddle" by* Nick Kershaw.

He pulled out a torch.

'I'm coming with you, and I'll shine the torch,' he said.

The three of them left through the up-and-over garage door and it came down hitting Lennard hard on the head.

'Oh-Ah!' he yelped and went berserk. After kicking a new dent into it and yelling to Jessy to stop barking up the lounge window he calmed down. Once he forced the door shut, they headed for Cotwall End. Lennard led a different way into the valley and crossed the stream using the footbridge made from railway sleepers.

'Here it is,' said Lucas as he pointed to the hole.

Lennard walked over and switched on the torch.

He shone it down into the dark pit,

'Well, look at that,' he said.

'What?' asked Robin anxiously.

'Don't be so nervous Boy!'

All three of them stood around and peered into the hole.

'Wow, seashells and pebbles,' said Lucas.

Lennard shone the torch all the way around thoroughly,

'Yeah, someone's stuck them into the side of the walls down there,' he said.

'Amazing,' said Robin, finding it hard to understand, scratching his head, 'I wonder where they came from.'

Lennard looked at Robin in disbelief, 'Well, I imagine from the sea,' he said.

Robin pulled a sad face.

'Yes, I know that I mean which seaside do you think they came from?'

Lennard Laughed, 'Well how should I know? Let's get back and fetch a Chinese, what do you reckon lads?' he asked.

'Why? Do you think he'll know where the shells came from?' asked Robin.

Lennard tumbled to the ground and began rolling around roaring with laughter. It was like he'd gone mad, Robin was worried, but Lucas seemed embarrassed.

Eventually, Lennard calmed down and got back to his feet. He continued as they began to walk home with broken laughter.

The three of them had reached Lucas's house.

They walked up to the front door with Lennard singing, "*These Boots Are Made for Walking*" By Lee Hazelwood and Nancy Sinatra.

Lucas's mom Sandra greeted them at the door,

'Where have you been?' she asked; 'you haven't been daft enough to go searching for fossils again have you? Just look at the state of you.'

'No, I wasn't, we found a deep hole in the ground with seashells grafted into the walls,' said Lennard.

'No! I found it first,' said Lucas.

'Yeah, yeah okay,' said Lennard.

'Oh no! You weren't stupid enough to go down it?' How did you end up in such a state?' she asked.

'It was this one here,' said Lennard as he pointed at Robin. 'I suggested fetching a Chinese and he only thought I meant to ask them where the seashells had come from.'

Lennard began to laugh again thinking about it.

'Oh!' said Sandra and contagiously began to laugh also. 'Don't,' she said. 'I've got a weak bladder,' and she had to make a mad dash to the toilet.

The following morning as Robin walked to school, he watched the birds fly across the clear blue sky. He could smell the scent of flowers as he passed the houses of well-maintained front gardens along the way. He came walking down in front of Lucas's Garden wall and saw Lennard hand the bucket of golf balls to Lucas from the garage. Robin waited for Lucas at the end of the driveway, 'Buzz off Bee!' he said with his arms in a flap. Lucas was ready and by the time the bumble bee had left Robin alone, he and Lucas headed to school.

'What were you jigging about the street for?' asked Lucas. 'Nothing' replied Robin bashfully.

'Didn't look like nothing.'

'Leave it, Lucas.'

They entered the school gates and Lucas took his football out of his backpack and kicked it into the playground. After having a kick about the school bells rang out and it was time to move inside.

Robin hung up his ruck sack in the cloakroom as usual taking only his pencil case and calculator into class with him.

Mrs McKay began to call the class register, but by the time she got to call Robin's name he had already lost concentration.

'Robin Butt!' she snapped sharply, 'Would you at least pay attention for once!' she cried.

Robin Jumped, 'Sorry Miss,' he said while scraping dirt from under his fingernail with his pencil.

'Here Miss,' he added, continuing to clean the rest of his fingernails.

'Yes, I should hope that I do know you're here by now, and will you at least pay attention in class for once? Always the boys,' she muttered.

Mrs McKay eventually completed filling in the class register.

'Everyone participating in *Midsummer Night's Dream*; I need you to go to the resource centre, take your scripts with you and get all of your costumes ready for the performance.'

She announced with authority as teachers do.

Robin was lucky, he never had lines to learn because his part was just a humble tree.

However, he knew everyone else's lines from all the rehearsing they'd done.

Mrs McKay hired an amateur film crew to film the play so that it would be available to buy on tape.

Because Robin knew this, he is excited to appear on television and has decided he would like to go into amateur dramatics and take acting seriously as a profession for when eventually he would have to get a job.

The performance involved a lot of work from everyone and was tiresome under the hot stage lights.

Year six was split into two groups and each group had their own set of the same characters, because of this it took the entire day to film. The end of the school day had come, Lucas fetched the bucket of golf balls from his locker after getting out of his horse costume and gave Robin the nod to get going. They headed on down to Mr Bourneview's office, when they arrived Lucas knocked on the newly re-placed door not noticing the wet paint notice that was now on the floor. Mr Bourneview had previously taped it to the wet door. Now Lucas had green paint all over his knuckles. 'Oh Pants!' he said, 'Why would you even try and tape a sign to wet paint like that?' he complained frustratedly picking it up from the floor.

'I don't know,' said Robin. 'Maybe because he's an academic man.'

Mr Bourneview answered the door and said, 'Right boys, are you ready to smash some balls?' he asked picking one out of Lucas's bucket. 'Blimey! These have seen some action, haven't they,' he said. 'Well, they ain't seen nothing yet.' and he put it back.

Lucas handed Mr Bourneview the ruined notice,

'Oh, cack!' said Mr Bourneview, 'who's done that?' he asked.

'You did,' said Lucas.

'Oh well, never mind,' said Mr Bourneview taking it from Lucas and putting it in the bin.

He picked up his golf bag from behind the door and brought it into the corridor. 'Here take these,' he said handing Robin a 460 Driver and Lucas another. Then he locked the door behind him and got paint on his tie.

'Oh, sod it!' he said irritably, 'You need to watch out for that bleeder.'

Mr Bourneview, Lucas and Robin walked down the corridor, through the old library, through to the empty dining hall, through the high spacious assembly hall into the infant's corridor, and then out onto the playground.

They climbed up the steep bank onto the flat and vast playing field.

'Okay,' said Mr Bourneview as he dropped his golf bag to the ground, then breathed back a deep breath of clean fresh air.

They stood still a moment, taking in the view of the surrounding trees, and golf course beyond.

'Well; come on lads let's get this thing started, go on you go first,' said Mr Bourneview to Robin.

Mr Bourneview pushed a tee into the ground and stepped back.

Robin took a ball from the bucket and placed it on the tee, he took a swing, hitting it a fair few meters up the field.

'Not bad Robin, not bad,' said Mr Bourneview, he then picked out a ball from the bucket and pushed a new tee into the ground.

Now watch this for some Drive!' he said.

He got into position, aimed and took a swing.

The golf ball exploded through the neighbouring kids' nursery with a smash.

'Blast,' he shouted.

'*OY*!!!' A loud voice came from the golf ball-sized hole in the broken window, it was an angry member of staff.

Mr Bourneview panicked.

'They can't know it was me, they just can't,' he cried!

'Wait!' screamed Lucas,

'There's no time!' yelped Mr Bourneview as he ran away.

'What do we do?' flapped Robin.

'Scatter!' Bourneview screeched from afar.

Mr Bourneview ran back towards the school.

He ran so fast he tripped over a lost dolly,

somersaulted over the brow of the hill and rolled down the embankment to the bottom of the Oak-tree.

Robin and Lucas ran the opposite way and through a hole in the boundary fence.

They burst into Lucas's back gate.

'What in the name of sanity! What's going on?' asked Lennard.

Lucas and Robin fought for their breath.

'Mr Bourneview-' Lucas gasped, 'smashed the nursery window.' he explained leaning down on his knees.

'Hang on? if he did that, why are you two so scared? And how did he smash the window in the first place?' asked Lennard waiting for the answer.

'We played golf on the school field,' said Robin.

'You might have,' said Lucas. 'I didn't even get to have a go did I.'

'Wait a minute lad, you can't play golf in the school field. Not without holes.'

'Well, there's a hole now,'

'Shut up Robin!' snapped Lucas.

'Flip me, boys! Just tell me what happened.'

'Well, we were just seeing how far we could smack our balls, it was the headmaster's idea,' said Robin.

'Yeah, it was his fault putting the window through like that,' said Lucas. Lennard rubbed his chin.

'We'll all right, but it doesn't seem very responsible of him to me. When you've both got your breath back, we can get an Indian,' said Lennard rubbing his hands together.

'Why? Do you think he will come and fix the window?'

'No Robin, *no*!' said Lennard.

'Hey, and where's the bucket of golf balls I gave you?'

'They could be anywhere by now,' said Lucas.

'What!'

'Well, our balls dropped and rolled down the road as we ran back.' Lennard sighed and shook his head. That evening Lucas decided to pitch his tent in the back garden as it was so hot. Robin helped as he was invited to stay over. Lennard bought the small TV from the garage for them. He plugged the extension reel into the shed, unwinding it to the tent's entrance.

'What if we get electric 'n' executed if it rains?' asked Lucas.

'Then it'll be goodnight and God bless mate,' said Lennard.

Lucas screamed and shouted for his mom. Sandra stuck her head out of the bathroom window wondering what all the commotion was about.

'Do you mind? I'm trying to unblock this plugger-hole up here!' she said.

'Plugger hole?' wondered Robin, 'She likes a drop, does she?' he asked turning to Lennard.

'She does actually,' replied Lennard. 'Madera to be frank'.

'What, you say?' she asked.

'*Nothing.*' Said Lennard. 'Lucas is worrying about getting electrocuted by the TV if it were to rain.

'Don't be stupid Lucas!' She snapped waving the plunger. 'It's not going to rain tonight.'

After flicking through the available five channels and talking about girls, it got late and Lucas switched off the TV, 'Oh, that's a right wrench of stench Robin!' he said, hiding away in his sleeping bag.

With the TV off it became very dark. Robin gazed up through the mesh vent in the tent roof up to the stars. He lay there for a while listening to the traffic from the main road. A black round object appeared above the mesh vent and suddenly, a huge bright light shone down. 'Were being abducted!' yelled Robin.

'Were being electrocuted!' screamed Lucas.

Lennard who was responsible was heard laughing outside and began to sing "A Spaceman Came Travelling" by Chris De Burgh.

'Get bent Dad,' said Lucas. Lennard laughed and whistled the theme tune to "The X-Files" as he headed back to the house.

It was a gorgeous and hot day the following day. Lucas unzipped the tent.

 'Wow! It stinks in here boys,' said Lennard as he stuck his head inside to greet them.

'Come to the kitchen, I've done egg and bacon Cobs for breakfast. Robin and Lucas vacated the tent and followed Lennard to the kitchen. 'How long are you planning on keeping that tent on my lawn?' he asked.

'Maybe the rest of summer,' replied Lucas. As the three of them sat at the kitchen bar and ate, Lennard began to sing, The Green, Green Grass of Home by Tom Jones, feeling sorry for himself. Robin and Lucas walked to school and had their usual kickabout in the playground before moving inside.

Later that day the classroom door opened. Everybody fell silent. Robin turned and noticed that a fresh-faced girl had entered the room with her mother. Mrs McKay greeted them and then showed them around the classroom ignoring the other pupils leaving them to do their work. Robin wondered and thought he'd better get back to doing his own.

During the lunch break, Robin and Lucas were having a kickabout.

For a moment Robin stopped, with the ball under one foot.

'Did you see that girl who entered our class earlier?' he asked.

'Yes, are you going to kick that ball?' asked Lucas as he parted his curtains, 'I think she's decided to come to this school,' he said.

'How would you know that?' asked Robin.

'Why else would she be shown the classroom like that?' said Lucas.

'Where do you suppose she's from?' asked Robin.

'How should I know? I guess it's somewhere sexy,' How can somewhere be sexy?' asked Robin.

'I wonder what her name is. Oh well, I think she's a babe anyway,' said Lucas stealing the ball from under Robin's foot.

'I suppose she was pretty,' said Robin.

Pretty! She was more than just pretty.

All right! Are you going to kick that ball now you've got it or what?' Asked Robin impatiently.

'Hey all right, calm down, don't get your knickers around the twist,' said Lucas, as he did a little dance. 'You're just excited about there being a chance that the girl might join our class, aren't you?' asked Robin, and with his left foot stole the ball back.

Lucas laughed knowing he knew Robin was spot on. 'Right, I'm going in for a goal now you big Jessy. watch this!'

Robin kicked the ball harder than ever, but his judgment was completely off.

It bounced off the goalpost and flew at two hundred miles per hour, which seemed to travel in slow motion according to Robin and Lucas. Now heading towards Mrs Eggbeater, it luckily only just missed her by an inch. She stood with a shocked expression on her face as it flashed passed. Still travelling at speed, it was now on a collision course towards Matt Tomlington who hadn't got a clue that the ball was heading straight for him.

His face disappeared behind the ball like a total eclipse. Robin and Lucas could only stand and watch as the ball struck him on the nose.

'Oh, that's it now, you're gonna be in so much trouble for that, exclaimed Lucas with panic on his face.

Matt Tomlington got himself up off the ground, dusted himself down, and returned to his feet. As others gathered around Matt, Robin began to panic. They pointed at Robin to show that he was the one who had kicked the ball. As soon as Matt realised it was Robin; he ran straight at him, smacking him on the nose.

'It was an accident. He didn't do it on purpose,' Stated Lucas, in defence of Robin who was now on his back.

Both Robin and Matt were escorted to Mr Bourneview's office, and Mr Bourneview phoned both their parents. Robin's mother Joan was called first.

'Well, kids will be kids at the end of the day won't they Mrs Butt.

Let's just put it down to an unfortunate accident. Don't worry, I won't take any further action against Robin, he has always been a good chap and I've made him shake Mathew Tomlington's hand and apologise to him,' thinking to himself that at least Robin hadn't broken a window as he had.

'Thank you, Mr Bourneview,' said Joan, 'And I will tell Robin to be more mindful when playing football with Lucas in future.'

'Once again, I apologise for having to call, goodbye and have a pleasant evening,' wished Mr Bourne-view. He came off the phone and put a pen between his teeth as he stared up the school drive to Longfel-low Road through his office window.

'Can we go now?' asked Robin.

'Oh yes, carry on boys,' said Mr Bourneview as he placed his pen down on the desk and swiftly moved over to the door to open it.

Chapter 2

LOVESTRUCK

Robin met Lucas in the school playground, 'How's your nose after yesterday?' asked Lucas. 'It hurts like a swine,' replied Robin holding his head in shame.

'Oh, that's too bad, Hey I saw that girl come into school just before you arrived,'

'You Did?' asked Robin.

'Yeah, I fancy her,' said Lucas as he smiled.

'Oh, really now? You don't wait for the shipping forecast do you,' said Robin jealously.

Lucas seemed as though he'd just seen the light. 'I hope to sing to her at break time,' he said.

Robin was gobsmacked because he had never known his friend to have such courage as this, especially with it being a girl he had never met before.

'So, what are you gonna do?' asked Robin curiously.

'To impress her, I'm going to find her on the playground at lunchtime and sing to her.'

'What are you going to sing?' asked Robin.

'I'm going to sing that song that's in the charts, *Rotterdam (or anywhere)* By the Beautiful South, everybody likes that song,' explained Lucas.

'Oh, no! thought Robin, 'He's serious about impressing her and if she does like him that means I've lost my best friend forever!'

Just as promised, Lucas found the new girl and sang to her in the playground during the lunchtime break. As he did so, she stood still with her hand over her mouth concealing a shy smile.

'Well, that's torn it,' said Robin out loud.

'Oh, do you like her too Robin?' Asked Mrs Button, the Dinner lady.

'No,' said Robin disappointedly. 'It's not that.'

He looked down at his polished shoes, staring at his reflection with disappointment on his face and feeling left out.

When school had finished, Robin rushed home to be back in time for Knightmare on television to cheer himself up.

Later that evening he went to his room and put a cassette tape mix into his stereo.

He picked up the book *"The Famous Five"* by Enid Blyton he had been given by Mr Bourneview and started reading. There was a knock at the front door, it was Lucas. Robin and Lucas usually called for each other spontaneously like this. Lucas brought his dog Jessy with him and asked if Robin would go searching for lost golf balls again. Of course, he wanted to, how could he turn down such an offer?

They walked down into Milton Crescent, which the school's playing field backed onto. There's a footpath that takes you there, around the outside of the perimeter fence which runs at the bottom of the golf course. From there, you can get inside by walking through the Badgers' set. You can smell the scent of cut grass and hear the spray of water sprinklers and tractor mowers. Sweat was dripping from both their faces, as it was so hot. Robin and Lucas were walking towards the small pond on hole three where Lucas began to tell Robin that he was going out with the new girl from school.

'I saw you sing to her,' said Robin. 'I couldn't do anything as brave as that.' Then he went on to ask, 'What's her name?'

'Robin! You're having a laugh. If you would listen, you would know,' Replied Lucas in disbelief.

'I don't know what you mean,' said Robin naively.

'What are you doing when the morning register is called?' asked Lucas.

'Looking out the window.' Replied Robin.

'Well, that says it all.'

'So, what's her name?'

'Seriously you don't know?'

'Yes_ I mean no'.

'It's Lauren,' Replied Lucas.

'Where are you going to take her?'

'What do you mean where am I going to take her?'

'You said you are going out with her.'

Lucas laughed, 'It's not going out like that,' he said.

'Oh, what do you mean then?

That doesn't make sense,' said Robin with confusion written all over his face.

Lucas smirked, 'You're joking, aren't you? you know, going out?

'Yes, going out for dinner,' said Robin.

'No, going out, *going out*!' said Lucas.

'You're kidding,' said Robin.

'No, I'm not kidding,' said Lucas teasingly.

'Well, if you're not going out, what does "going out" mean then?

Lucas paused, he stopped walking and went on to explain.

'It's when you see each other and go on walks, talk, kiss and just spend time with each other as Boy-friend and girlfriend.'

'Oh right,' said Robin as they continued to walk.

'So that's what it means,' he thought, leaving him fantasizing about what going out with someone is really like. The thought of it was exciting as he gazed at the rolling clouds up above the treetops. Not more than a moment later he began to think that he had never experienced anything like that before and that he had no one to share all those things with anyway, nor know anyone he would want to either.

This left him believing that he was losing the race and getting left behind. Not that it was a race, he just wanted to feel the thrill with someone and feel it right now.

'I would have expected you to have known what going out meant already,' said Lucas as he let Jessy off the lead.

'Well, I don't talk to girls much, do I?' replied Robin feeling a little foolish and picked a dandelion from the ground.

'Hey, you can take her stickleback fishing, she might like that,' suggested Robin as he blew dandelion seeds everywhere.

'Don't be daft, I am not doing that with her,' said Lucas.

'I thought that would be a good icebreaker,' said Robin disappointedly.

'Trust me, Lauren isn't going to want to do that with me, that's for kids, and she'll find it boring.' Lucas picked up a stick and threw it for Jessie, 'You can stick your sticklebacks,' he said. He and Robin both laughed. 'If dogs could laugh Jessy would too,' said Robin. Lucas looked at Robin as if he were some kind of fool.

By now they had reached the pond and there were bushes and brambles all around.

Jessie disappeared into the overgrowth, the vegetation shook with agitation, and she re-emerged with a golf ball in her mouth.

Lucas ran over to her, and she turned her head and looked back at Robin.

Robin couldn't stop laughing.

'That's it, Jessie, you're a smart dog,' said Lucas as he wondered what Robin had found so funny.

'Drop it then,' he said. She dropped the ball for him, and he gave her a dog biscuit as a reward.

'What's so funny?' he asked smiling and expecting to hear something hilarious.

'She looked like she was laughing, that's all.'

'Stupid!' Lucas's smile turned to a glare.

'Hey if you show Lauren, Jessie doing that, she'll be impressed won't she,' said Robin.

'Well, better that than stickle backing,' said Lucas.

Robin and Lucas had collected a fair amount of golf balls and decided to call it a day. They took them back to Lucas's house and stored them in the garage.

Mr Bourneview took the history lesson the next day. 'Right, we've studied Ironbridge already, and last week we learned about the history of the Straits House, so I suppose; ah yes we can have the Crooked House as our subject this week,' he said as he flicked through his notes.

'The Crooked House was first built in 1765 and was a farmhouse, it hasn't always been crooked, mind. So, who can tell me how the Crooked House became crooked?'

'An earthquake?' asked Ben.

'No, it wasn't an earthquake,' said Mr Bourneview.

'A cannon and ball from Dudley castle?' asked Mary.

'No! Most definitely not was it a cannonball,' said Mr Bourneview, in astonishment. 'How would it have retravelled that far anyhow?' he asked.

'Downhill!' shouted Steve.

'Yes, we'll all be going downhill at this rate,' said Mr Bourneview.

'Come on everyone, what did we cover on our local history a few weeks ago?' he asked.

'Yes Robin, you can put your hand down now.'

'Land mines!'

'What! No,' said Mr Bourneview.

'Sorry I mean from mines; this place is riddled with them all over this land.'

Mr Bourneview flinched with appraise, 'Yes, that's right Robin,' he said in a patronising manner.

'Coal and Iron ore mines caused the subsidence,' he explained.

'Well done, Robin' he said. 'At least someone was paying attention. Which house group are you in?'

Mr Bourneview was about to peel a tiny yellow sticker from the merit pack and award it to Robin's house group.

'Kinver Sir.'

Mr Bourneview peeled the sticker and stuck it to the Kinver column on the merit board.

'Sir?'

'Yes Ben,' replied Mr Bourneview.

'How come Clent house group doesn't have that many merits?'

'Well, I guess you'll just have to earn more won't you my boy,' said Mr Bourneview.

'Sir?' asked Ben a second time.

'*Yes,*' replied Mr Bourneview tiresomely.

'Is the Straits House called Straits because it's not crooked like the Crooked one?' Ben asked trying to earn a merit also.

'No Boy! It is not,' answered Mr Bourneview.

And if we keep this nonsense up, we'll just have to start deducting merits, won't we?' he added.

'Oh, but Sir, there's only one up there as it is,' said Ben in disappointment.

'Look here, I say. You'll just need to be a little bit smarter won't you dear boy,' explained Mr Bourneview.

'Oh, stuff it then!' said Ben irritably.

'What! How dare you boy!' shouted Mr Bourneview. 'Right, you're not even gonna have any at all,' he boomed.

Mr Bourneview tried to scratch the remaining merit from the Clent column off, but it wasn't coming away. He punched the board hurting his fist, and then in a fit of rage he ripped the whole thing off the wall taking the plaster with it. And then he pounced on it. 'Oh no, my merit,' cried Robin.

Mr Bourneview calmed down and looked at the smashed board under his feet.

Mr Bourneview apologised, 'Oh, Sorry Robin,' he said,

'We need more stickers. "Ben!" 'Go round Megg's corner shop and buy more,' he demanded.

Mr Bourneview spent the rest of the afternoon trying to fix the house merit board but failed and ended up supergluing his tie to it.

The school bell rang for home time and the class was dismissed. Robin packed his backpack, fought through the overcrowded corridor and walked around to his great-uncle Jack's house, which was just around the corner. Previously the washing line prop had fallen and gone through his greenhouse, and Jack snapped it into three pieces in temper.

Robin rang the doorbell but there was no answer. He tried the side gate, it was open, so Robin walked through to the back garden and saw Jack picking up the pieces of snapped line prop.

'Are you all right Jack?'

'Yes, I'm fine thanks Robin,'

'Shall I call the police?'

'No Robin, why call the police?' asked Jack tying the prop back together with industrial tape.

'Well, you've been broken into from the look of it,' said Robin.

'No, the line prop broke the greenhouse,' explained Jack.

'Oh, right. But how did the line prop get broken? And into all those pieces?' asked Robin. 'Did the greenhouse cut it to pieces?' he added.

'Oh, the prop; yes, the greenhouse did it,' said Jack as he continued to fix it.

Some weeks had passed.

Robin and Lucas were still close friends as they always had been, considering Lucas was spending more time with Lauren now. Apart from having an interest in finding lost golf balls, Robin and Lucas shared an interest in music as well.

They were at Lucas's house and having a good old jam on his keyboard.

It was a sleek and versatile instrument of its time that could produce a variety of sounds and rhythms. Lucas had been playing the keyboard since he was very young, and he had a natural talent for it.

He could play any song he heard, and he also composed some of his tunes. He loved to show off his skills to Robin, who was always impressed by his musical abilities.

This evening, Lucas was showing Robin a new song he had learnt to play. It was a catchy pop song that had been topping the charts for weeks. Lucas played the melody with his right hand and the chords with his left hand while singing along with the lyrics.

He looked at Robin with a smile, inviting him to join in. Robin pretended to grab a microphone and sang the chorus with him. They sounded great together and had a lot of fun.

After they had finished the song, Lucas asked Robin if he wanted to try playing anything else. Robin hesitated because he didn't know how to read music.

He'd never taken any formal lessons but agreed to give it a go.

Lucas showed him how to position his fingers on the keys, but Robin felt more comfortable placing them his way.

Lucas played the song again, slowly and clearly, so that Robin could see which keys were struck.

Robin watched carefully, trying to memorise the sequence of notes. He also listened closely, because he had a sharp ear for sound, even though he didn't realise it.

Robin tried to play the song after Lucas had finished. He pressed the keys one by one, following the melody as best he could. He made some mistakes along the way, but he didn't give up. He hit the wrong note at one point, but he thought the combination sounded like *"Brother Louie"* by Modern Talking, and he played what sounded natural to him. He added some extra notes and chords, creating his version of the song.

Lucas was amazed by what he heard. He couldn't believe that Robin could play so well, without any sheet music or guidance. He stopped Robin and asked him how he did it.

'I just guess how the music should sound,' he said casually.

'Wow, that's ace!' Lucas gave Robin a high-five and praised him for his talent. They didn't realise how late it was until Sandra came downstairs and told them to wrap it up.

The next school day Robin and Lucas were on their way to school. Lucas began to tell Robin that he was writing a song for Lauren, as they both walked together.

'You never mentioned this last night,' said Robin in astonishment.

'No, I produced it when I was in bed. I will show you how far I've got with it later if you like.'

Poor Lucas had a ridiculously gruelling day at school from the outset. He forgot to bring in his maths homework, which was most likely to do with Lauren's song on his mind. He got in trouble with Mrs Spencer. He felt ashamed and embarrassed, especially because Lauren saw the whole ordeal.

Later, Lucas accidentally dropped his science project in the corridor and got trampled on by the other pupils. He had worked hard on it for weeks, but now it has dusty footprints all over. He felt angry and frustrated yet again, especially when Lauren saw the mess and tried to console him. He ran away hiding in the toilets, thinking that she would be pitying him by now.

'What a way to lose your dignity,' he thought.

Then he realised that he had left his English essay in the library, which another pupil had stolen, yet he was to know. He had written a brilliant essay on his favourite book, "*Five Children and It*" by Edith Nesbit, but now it was gone. He felt hopeless and depressed, especially when Lauren found out about it. She offered to give him another essay at home she could spare. He accepted her offer but was not happy with all that had happened throughout the day.

And so, he missed every opportunity to spend time with Her, in avoiding her. He thought that he had failed at everything and that she was too smart for him.

He headed straight home after school, miserable and lonely. Robin was not far behind, knowing that he needed a friend right now. Robin couldn't keep up; he didn't get out of school as quickly, held up in the crowd. He watched as Lucas let himself in the front door. Robin knocked on it when he got there, and Sandra answered. 'Oh, I'm glad you've come,' she said gratefully. 'Come in, I take it Lucas has had a bad day, he hasn't said a word and has gone straight to his room.' Robin went upstairs and gently tapped the bedroom door. There was no answer, so he let himself in any way. He found Lucas lying on his bed, staring at the ceiling.

'Hey, are you okay?' he asked.

'Terrible, I've had the worst day ever. I ruined my science project, lost my essay, forgot my Maths homework and throughout it all, I've made a fool of myself in front of Lauren.'

'I wouldn't worry about that; I'm sure she doesn't think any different of you.'

I'm worthless,' said Lucas. Robin wasn't convinced and believed Lucas was being a little over dramatic.

'Hey! Don't say that. You're not worthless, you're just human. We all make mistakes, just take Mr Bourneview.'

'But I make too many mistakes. I can't do anything right. I can't even talk to Lauren after what's happened today.'

'Lucas, don't you think you're being a bit too hard on yourself? You're a smart, talented, kind person. You have so many good qualities and you are more confident than I am, and you have a good sense of humour. I would rather be in your shoes.

'Really?'

'Yeah, Lauren would love it if she got to know you better, I reckon. You're funny. You always make me laugh with your jokes and pranks.'

'Thanks, but that's not enough to impress Her. She's so beautiful and smart and cool.'

'You're also creative. You have a great imagination when it comes to music, and you write amazing songs.'

'Thanks, said Lucas.

'You're also a good friend. You're always there for me when I need you. You're a true friend,' said Robin.

'Thanks for that Robin.'

Robin began to sing, "*With a Little Help from My Friends*" by The Beatles, and Lucas joined in. Afterwards, Lucas got up and opened his window, 'I Like to feel the breeze flow through the room this time of year,' he said.

'That's more like it,' said Robin, 'Now let's hear this song you're writing for Lauren.'

'All right, what if she hates it though?'

'And what if she loves it?'

'Then I'll be the happiest person in the world,' said Lucas.

'Exactly! So, let's hear this song you wrote for her.'

'Okay, I'll show you.' Lucas headed downstairs to the lounge with Robin following. Lucas set up the keyboard and began to play, he played a little introduction and started to sing about Lauren.

Lennard shouted over from the armchair putting his newspaper down, and Lucas stopped.

'Hey Lad, don't go rubbing it in, you know that Robin doesn't have a girlfriend yet.'

Lucas looked at Robin and then turned to Lennard. 'Oh, he's all right, he wants to hear this song anyway,' he said.

'Robin was secretly yearning to experience having a girlfriend; Lucas continued to play.

'You can't do that,' said Lennard.

'Why not?' asked Lucas.

'Why? It sounds like "*Everywhere*" by Fleetwood Mac, that's why. You can't rip off "Fleetwood Mac", you'll have to make your own.'

'Fine!' said Lucas.

Lucas began to play again, 'You can't do that either,' said Lennard.

'Oh! What now?' asked Lucas.

'Now you're doing "*Together, We'll Be Ok*" by Cannon and Ball, that's what.'

Lucas huffed, 'Right, how about this?'.

He began to play again, and this time with a new arrangement of notes.

'Ah, Yes, that's much better,' said Lennard. 'You can't use music that's not your own.'

And as that was said Lennard began to sing, "*Make Your Own Kind of Music,*" by Mama Cass Elliot, (1969).

'Can't that wait until I'm finished?' sneered Lucas.

Lennard muttered, 'Kids these days, don't know good taste even when it slaps em in the chops!'

He picked up his newspaper and snapped the pages. Robin listened to Lucas's song while imagining sharing his own life with a girl of his own, a girl who supports his passions and dreams. As the song continued, he imagined holding her and kissing beneath a grand Oak tree in the summer sun. He felt empty, the colour drained from his face as he broke into a hot sweat. He hopes to find the one sometime soon; his soulmate, someone who will make him happy and complete. Yearning, pining to spend time with a special someone before the summer's out. He continued to think and thought about the dark Winter nights and the icy blast that comes with them. He thought about the Autumn and Bonfire night and the smell of spent fireworks. 'Maybe it's just as romantic without the summer sun?' he wondered.

'You look sad Robin,' said Sandra.

'I'm sure you'll find the one soon enough,' she said, continuing to read her magazine.

'Yeah, you will mate; a nice one, just like mine,' said Lucas as he finished playing his song. 'Well, what did you think?'

'It's great, made me think,' said Robin. Lucas's face beamed. 'Great! Now, time to hear me play *"Miami Vice"* by Jan Hammer.'

Sandra peered over her glasses towards him.

'All right mate, stop showing off,' she said.

'Oh, to be in love and feel its short sharp crack.' sighed Lennard.

'Well, at least he's cheered up now,' said Sandra.

Lucas had a sense of bewilderment come over him.

'What do you mean dad? Does love sting?'

'You'll find out when she chucks Ya.'

'Hey Dad, that's a horrible thing to say.'

'Yeah, that's a bit harsh even for you Lennard.' said Sandra.'

'*Well*, he knows I'm just pulling his leg, but just watch out, I say; she'll soon get bored with watching you play your computer games and all that plinky-plonky on the honky-tonky.'

Lucas suddenly slammed the keys down hard.

'Forget it!' he said, 'Come on Robin, let's go get some balls.'

Lennard tumbled out of his armchair to the floor and began roaring with laughter and Lucas slammed the front door on the way out.

("Well! That's torn it!") It read on page five of Lennard's newspaper which was seen through the ripped hole of page three. Lennard laughed even harder, and Sandra just shook her head.

'I thought your song was amazing, Lauren is going to love it,' Robin said joyfully.

'Thanks, and I hope you're right,' said Lucas.

The next school day in the music lesson Lucas turned on the keyboard which stood proudly on its stand in the corner of the room. Since Mrs Singer was having a natter with Mrs Spinster in the opposite classroom, Lucas got everybody's attention by banging the drum. 'Lauren!' he called. 'This song is for you.' The whole class fell silent, there was the distant short laugh of someone in the background. Lucas began to play Lauren's song, and the class began to laugh except for Robin and Lauren. Lauren stared in awe of him playing her song and she loved every bit of it. Mrs Singer came back into the classroom, 'What the! Who said you could- Oh, what a beautiful piece of music,' she said. 'Carry on, it's lovely. This is the best thing since "*Words*", by F. R David.'

The others were no longer laughing. When Lucas finished the song, Mrs Singer clapped and so did everyone else; there was a massive roar of clapping and cheering, and even Mrs Spinster came in to see what the commotion was all about.

Once school was over Lauren found Lucas and Robin sitting in the shade under the old oak tree. She walked over and sat next to Lucas. Robin walked away to leave them both alone, neither did he call for Lucas that evening either.

It was sports day the next day, Robin and Lucas carried their chairs from the classroom to the playing field with the rest of the school pupils.

Watching others race around the racetrack, Robin was losing his patience with his chair, since the legs kept sinking into the ground and he was having to keep pulling it back out again.

Lucas sat next to Lauren, pulling faces at Robin from the other side of the running track, so Robin gave him the V sign.

Lauren pulled a shocked face; Robin was escorted to the headmaster's office by Mrs Treadmill.

'Why do they call it the V sir?' asked Robin curiously.
'Why do you ask that?' asked Mr Bourneview.
'Well, I think it should be called the Y,' said Robin.
'Why?' asked Mr Bourneview.
'Well, it looks like a Y with your arm included, doesn't it?'
'Okay now Robin, just finish your lines so that we can get out of here sooner.'

Chapter 3

SCHOOLS OUT

It's Thursday *20th June 1997*, and it's another hot day. Robin called in for Lucas on the way to school that morning. Lennard made them a cup of tea and offered biscuits on a plate. 'How do you feel about it being the last day of school?' he asked.

Robin stared through the back patio doors into the garden. 'Strange,' he said.

Lennard joined Robin in looking at the garden.

'Yeah, it's strange for me too; growing up fast, aren't we?' He said with a sense of sadness.

'I didn't realise how weird it would be until now that we are leaving,' said Lucas.

On their way out, Robin glanced at the new wallpaper in the hallway.

'Do you like my updated wallpaper?' asked Lennard trying to cheer them all up.

'Yes, I think it's Ace,' said Robin as he moved in for a closer look. The wallpaper was a pattern of various tropical fruits.

'If you lick the fruit on the paper, you will get a taste of it, it's tasty wallpaper just like in *"Charlie and The Chocolate Factory"* by Roald Dahl,' said Lennard.

So, Robin licked a pineapple. 'I can't taste that one,' he said.

Lennard pointed at the coconut, 'Oh, how about this one?' he said.

'No, nothing!' replied Robin.

Lucas sniggered and looked at Lennard and Lennard Laughed, 'Go on, you can't be late on your last day,' he said as he encouraged both Robin and Lucas out of the front door.

The two of them walked down to the bottom of the drive.

'Your dad's a comic isn't he,' said Robin.

'Ha- I can't believe you licked the wallpaper,' said Lucas. 'I wondered how long it would be until you realised that he was joking,' he said, leaving Robin feeling stupid.

'I'm surprised you can't taste wallpaper paste.'

Lauren was just getting out of her mother's car as Robin and Lucas were nearby. They were a few yards from the school gate, Lucas ran up to her and threw his school bag to the ground. Robin could only watch as he wondered what the heck was going on! Lauren smiled at Lucas as he hurtled towards her. A car drove passed with its windows down, *"Drive"* by The Cars, was on the radio, and could be heard as the car drove all down the road. He then grabbed hold of her once he was at arm's reach. He pulled her toward him and kissed her on the mouth. Robin was shocked.

'I can't believe those two did that, right in front of her mom and everyone like that. I wish I could do that too if only I had a girlfriend.'

'Now pick that bag up! You silly little boy. I almost tripped over that.'

'It isn't mine,' replied Robin to a very angry lady who was walking by. 'I suppose I've got to take this in for him now,' he thought.

What a sad and surreal feeling it was, to have heard Mrs McKay call out the register to year six for the very last time. Everyone had brought chocolates and cakes to share, except for the boys who had climbed the school roof, they were expelled yesterday.

Mrs McKay asked if anyone would like to share a memorable moment that they had in the time they spent at Longfellow & Shakespeare Primary, so Robin put his hand in the air.

'Yes Robin,' she said as she was unexpectedly but joyfully surprised. 'Come up to the front.' Everyone gasped because Robin had always been shy and had always lacked confidence when having the centre of attention. Because it was the last day, he didn't care and walked to the front anyhow. He cleared his throat.

'Erm; *There once was a Primary called Long and Shaky,
it wasn't much fun and the dinners were flaky,*'

'Erm, Robin, I guess that's enough, go and sit back
down.' The class was shocked by Robin's antic.
Throughout most of his school years, he had been
shy and reserved. Everyone started chanting,

'*Robin, -Robin, -Robin, -Robin*'!

Robin grinned from all the attention and sat back
down next to Lucas. Lucas looked at Robin with a
half-surprised, half-impressed expression on his
face.

'I can't believe you got up and said that' he said.

Other members of year six got up and made a
speech as they reflected on the time that they had
spent at the school together, and later played board
games.

When the time came when it was near the end of the
last day, they all began to sign each other's school
uniform shirts.

Mrs Singer came into the classroom to see the current year six for the last and final time. She had also
brought in with her, her acoustic guitar.

'Mrs Singer?' asked Lucas, 'Please may we hear one of your songs before we leave school for the last time? A tear trickled down her cheek as she replied, 'Of course, that's why I have my guitar with me. I've written a song for you all as you've been such a pleasure to teach this year. Would you like to hear it?'

The whole of Year six shouted "YEAH!"

'Oh, bless you, she said as she began tuning her guitar. 'I'm going to miss all of you very much. You're the best students I've had in my music lessons since the 80s, so this song is for all of you. It's called school leavers of nineteen ninety-seven.'

Mrs Singer began playing her guitar and singing her song. The song sounded pretty much like a cross between country and folk music. You could also hear that the tune sounded a little bit like, *"You Can Do Magic"* by America *(1982)*. Robin and Lucas decided to take a final look at the school they had attended for the last five years.

At 15:30 the school bells rang out, and Mrs McKay wished everyone well for the future. All the girls wept, and the clock dropped off the wall. Finishing school for the last time was hard to understand and come to terms with according to Robin.

Robin, Lucas, Lauren, Kate, Lori and Richard met on the school's playing field after leaving their classroom for the last time.

The sun was beating down, and Lucas fetched a picnic blanket from home. He placed it in the partial shade of the silver birch which stood on the banked perimeter. He and Lauren lay on it, gazing up into the sky.

'Remember all those times we've played in this field?' asked Robin sadly.

'Yeah, I can't believe we'll never go back to Longfellow ever again,' said Kate.

'No, I can't either, it's kind of sad, isn't it,' said Lauren as she gazed above the fir trees.

'It'll be cool to meet new people though' she added.

Lori was sitting on the grass, she looked up at Robin, 'That was great earlier when you said the school wasn't much fun and the dinners were flaky,' she said laughing.

Lucas looked at Lauren, and then back at Robin.

'Yeah, that was brilliant; you should have done more things like that, you might even have been more popular over the years,' he said.

'I can't believe you've finally come out of your shell,' said Richard.

'I can't believe, I can't believe, that's all I've been hearing lately,' said Robin, he never cared about being popular anyway but was pleased to feel more confident.

After a couple more hours of reminiscing, everyone decided it was time to wrap it up and go home.

Robin wasn't ready to go yet and asked Lucas if he could borrow the picnic blanket just for a short while and give it back on his way home. Everyone went their separate ways leaving Robin behind. Lucas and Lauren left together, and Robin was left there alone. Kate was last to leave as she left through the top gate, then turned and looked back towards Robin, and continued out. There was the sound of the wind through the trees and the chip of someone hitting the odd golf ball, even a hot-air balloon drifted overhead.

Now that everyone had gone it had become a lonely place.

After around forty minutes of listening to Bliss, Robin's eyes became heavy, and he fell asleep in the cool shade.

Chapter 4
THE HUNGRY EYES

Robin's uncle Dave had booked a caravan holiday in Norfolk for the school holidays.

Robin is looking forward to going, he hasn't been on a caravan holiday since, well a very long time.

He is staying with his mom, Uncle Dave, Sister Jane, and Cousin Lucy. Robin's dad Brien can't stay though, as he can't get the time off work.

Robin headed down to call for Lucas, but Lucas wasn't allowed out because he'd swore at Lennard, so Robin decided to visit his great-uncle Jack instead.

Before Robin had a chance to knock on the door, Jack answered.

'Oh, hello Robin, come on in,' he said.

Jack was always pleased to have visitors.

Mr Thatcher, Jack's neighbour was in the lounge drinking tea at the time and from one of Jack's best China teacups.

There was enough tea left for another, so Jack poured one for Robin.

'How are you, Robin?' he asked.

'I'm all right Jack, thanks' said Robin.

Robin sat in the armchair opposite Mr Thatcher and Jack sat on the settee.

'How are you, young man,' asked Mr Thatcher, 'Still on the busses?'

'No, he's still at school, aren't you Robin,' said Jack.

'Yes, I'm still at school, Well I'll be going up to secondary school soon anyway,' said Robin.

'Ah yes, the best days of your life they are, the best days,' said Mr Thatcher finishing his tea.

Mr Thatcher pulled himself up out of his chair awkwardly, using his stick.

'Would you like another cup?' asked Jack.

'No, I don't think so, thank you, one's just enough for me. What shall I do with this cup?' he asked while examining it.

'I don't mind, do what you like with it,' said Jack.

Mr Thatcher tossed it into the fireplace with a deafening blast, Robin jumped out of his skin and began to hear a loud ringing in his ears.

Robin looked at Jack, but Jack shook his head discreetly to stop Robin from saying anything.

'I'll see myself out,' said Mr Thatcher.

Mr Thatcher closed the front door behind him.

'I can't believe he threw the cup in there like that,' said Robin in surprise.

'It's all right son,' said Jack, 'The war turned his mind.'

'Really? How come?' asked Robin.

'War is a terrible thing, Robin; it can break the best of men.'

'What causes wars?' asked Robin.

'It's when going to the pub isn't enough and they want to rule the world,' said Jack angrily.

'I'd much prefer to go to the pub,' said Robin.

'Me too,' said Jack. 'Here, tell you what, I'll make us a nice shandy but don't tell your dad.'

Jack went to the kitchen and poured half a can of bitter into each glass and topped them with cloudy lemonade.

'Shall I clean up this broken cup?' asked Robin.

'No, sod it!' said Jack.

That night was the night before the holiday and Robin had gone to a family party. Jack didn't go, he stayed in to watch the snooker.

The most memorable music you've ever heard was playing, it was the Nineties after all!

Robin's cousin Andy came over and spoke.

'We've got a table, come and join us.' A little later Robin was hyper from all the caffeine he had consumed from drinking fizzy pop. He asked his dad Brien if he could have a shandy, and Brien said.

'Yeah,' and got him lemonade.

Robin now believes he's drunk on shandy and is showing off on the dance floor, 'Are there any girls at your school that you fancy?' asked Andy as he tried to distract Robin from making a further fool of himself.

'No, there isn't. There's no one interested in me, and it's too late even if there were because I've left school anyway,' said Robin pitifully.

'That one over there keeps looking over, maybe you should go over and ask her out,' said Andy.

Robin gasped! 'She's way too young! And she could be related.'

'No, she's not related to us, and she looks about your age.'

'No, she's not my age,' said Robin in offence.

Andy laughed 'OK if you say so.'

'How do you impress girls anyway?' asked Robin.

'Can you make them laugh?' asked Andy.

'Yes, but I don't think it's in a good way,' said Robin.

Andy laughed, 'I'm sure it is. You just need to have a bit more faith in yourself,' he said.

Robin thought to himself, it must be so cool to be confident like Andy and know how to talk to girls.

The DJ began to play slow songs as it was near the end of the party. Mainly couples were dancing with each other to the music.

Andy thought Robin seemed unhappy.

'Are you all, right?' he asked. 'You look sad,' he added. Robin sighed,

'I'm OK, I just wanted someone to dance with,' he said.

'You should have talked to that one I mentioned earlier,' said Andy.

'Oh yeah, that one who's now asleep on her dad's lap!' said Robin as he pointed at her.

Andy turned and saw that Robin wasn't joking.

'I guess you were right,' said Andy.

'Oh well, you'll probably meet someone when you least expect it,' he added.

The party ended and Robin said goodbye to Andy. He left and walked home with his parents, wondering if he would ever find love. When he got home, he put on his headphones and a cassette tape mix of his favourite songs and lay down on his bed, he closed his eyes and tried to take his mind off finding love and all of that.

Chapter 5

DRIVE

The next day, Robin and his family packed their bags and got ready to go on their holiday to Norfolk. Robin was very excited about the trip, as he thought there would be much to do there but wasn't looking forward to the long drive. He doesn't like long car journeys, as they make him feel sick and find them boring. He got into the back seat of the car with his younger sister, who was annoying him with her constant chatter. His parents turned up the radio. He put on his headphones and tried to block out the noise with his portable cassette tape player. He looked out of the window and watched the scenery pass by, he wished he was at the caravan site already.

He wondered how long it would take to get there, all there was to do was, listen to the Radio and gaze out the window.

Robin and his family finally arrived at the caravan park after a long and boring drive. Brien had accidentally driven into the wrong site and had to turn around and find the right one. Brien was frustrated and tired and just wanted to drop them off and go back home. Because he had to work the next day and could not join them for the holiday Robin saw the disappointment in his face. "*Here Comes Summer*" by Jerry Keller was playing on the radio at the time. Brien turned off the ignition, the car shuddered and along with the radio came to silence.

Robin and his dad unloaded their bags and entered the caravan that Dave had rented.

It was wide and spacious and had everything that anyone could wish for. It had a kitchen, a toilet and shower, a living room, and two bedrooms.

Robin had the one bedroom all to himself and moved his belongings into it. He sat on the bed looking out of the window for a moment before unpacking his things. He unpacked his clothes along with a book called "The Armageddon Stratagem" and put them in a drawer. He didn't bring much away with him, as he thought there would be plenty of other interesting things to do there. He could hear Jane and Lucy next door through the thin wall, they were excited about sharing a bunk bed. He watched through the window as other people walked by. A girl cycling her bike rode passed, Robin saw her face as she turned back, which made him feel his face go hot. Then he got his book back out of the drawer and started reading to take his mind off her.

After a few hours, Brien decided it was a good time to go home. He said goodbye to them all unlocking the car, which was parked outside the caravan.

'Have a good time,' he said. 'And Give me a phone call in the week.' He got into the car and wound the window down, asking Robin to look after his sister and his cousin, to give his mother and uncle a break. Robin nodded and promised he would.

He watched as his dad drove away, feeling a pang of disappointment.

Once Robin settled in, which did not take him long, his little sister and cousin came knocking on the door. They wanted to go and play in the play area that was in the caravan park. It had swings, slides, seesaws, and a climbing tower. Robin did not want to go, but his mom told him to take them and keep a close eye on them. She suggested that he might make new friends, or at least have fun. Robin sighed. 'All right', he said. He put on his jacket and followed his sister and cousin outside.

He took them to the play area, which was surrounded by a picket fence. Kids were running around, and Robin felt out of place, as he felt he was much too old for this kind of thing.

He just sat on a swing watching his sister and cousin play. They seemed to be having a great time, but Robin was bored.

He looked around and noticed the girl with the bike again, who unknowing to him was the same age. She rode her bike around the outside of the play area. Robin wondered if she was about his age,

'Maybe a bit older,' he wondered.

She had long brown hair that flew behind her as she pedalled fast. She wore earrings and had sunglasses on top of her head, she looked cool.

Robin felt a twinge of envy as he watched her.

He wished he had brought his mountain bike with him, so he could ride with her or at least show off his skills. He loved riding his bike, especially on rough terrain like in the woods in Baggeridge Park, (South Staffordshire).

He watched her cycle for a while and boom! Electricity in his mind took hold of his body. That was until she saw him looking and looked back at him.

Robin felt his face heat up and quickly looked away. He felt embarrassed that she had caught him watching her. He wondered what she thought of him.

He wished he could talk to her but didn't know how to.

He was shy and felt awkward around girls, especially ones like her.

He decided to try and ignore her, focusing on keeping watch of Jane and Lucy and just being on holiday instead.

Jane and Lucy came to him, and he offered to push them on the swings.

He began to have fun pushing them simultaneously, but he couldn't get the girl out of his mind. His imagination took hold and wished he was somewhere else, somewhere more fun and exciting, somewhere with the girl, riding with her on the bike.

He managed to shrug the teasing thoughts out of his mind and eventually took Jane and Lucy back to the caravan.

Bewdleydale was on TV, Dave made his arm like a shotgun and sounded a fake blast when Tim Kate came on.

Robin sat on his bed reading The Armageddon stratagem. Passing the window, the girl rode by and distracted him from reading.

'I wish I had my bike here too,' he thought. She rode by again.

'She's so cute; No, I'm on holiday, Forget it.'

'Right, everyone! Let's go out in the car and get the best seaside fish and chips,' said Dave as his voice was heard through the walls from the kitchen.

'Yes! Fish and chips,' said Robin.

He jumped up off the bed nearly hitting the ceiling.

He flew out of his room and slipped on the kitchen floor, landing on his back. Joan and Dave laughed so hard that it took a while for them to get their breath back. Dave said it looked like something from a cartoon, where their legs were running in mid-air, and to be fair, Robin saw the funny side too.

Robin watched the sunset as he ate his fish and chips on the Hunstanton Seafront.

'What an amazing place,' he said. Uncle Dave agreed, 'Yeah, not bad, is it? We used to come here when we were children.'

'Well, how old are you now?' asked Robin.

'Ooh, I'm forty-three you bleeder!' said Dave, flicking Robin's ear.

Monday 28/07/1997

Awakened by a bicycle bell outside, Robin rubbed his eyes, it was a nice sunny day to wake up to again. 'Someone else is up already,' he thought. He heard Dave as he closed the fridge door. Robin got out of bed and got dressed, made himself a bowl of cereal and watched television.

The smoke alarm started blaring off because Joan had burned some toast!

'Wow, that's loud in a caravan,' shouted Robin.

'Yeah, one million decibels,' shouted Dave with his fingers in his ears.

He wafted the smoke detector with the washing-up towel.

'Ouch! Why does it have to be so loud?' asked Robin.

'It's supposed to be this loud if there's a fire, you silly little sod,' said Dave.

After the alarm was silenced, the car alarm started going off.

'Oh right, now it's your turn, is it? Shouted Dave irritably. He rummaged through his fleece quickly and snatched the car keys from one of the pockets in a faff. 'We'll end up bleeding evicted!' he said.

Robin and Joan smirked as they thought Dave's way of expressing himself wasn't half funny at times,

'What do you reckon about seeing the beach?' Dave asked, after

silencing the car alarm.

'Oh, yes! let's go see the sea,' said Robin excitedly.

Everybody got ready and headed for the beach, which was just outside of the caravan park. While taking a walk along the beach, Dave said to watch out for dog eggs.

'Dog Eggs? What are Dog Eggs?' asked Robin curiously.

'Dog Muck Boy!' replied Dave.

'Oh no, it's everywhere here!' said Robin as he picked up a pebble.

'What are you doing with that?' asked Dave. 'The tides far out you silly shrimp,' he said.

'It's not for throwing in the sea,' replied Robin as he threw it straight at some Dog poo.

'It's meant to kill those flies that were on that dog muck,' he said. The flies flew up in the air and Dave couldn't stop laughing, and neither could Joan. 'You, silly little turd-fly,' said Dave as he lost his footing and fell to the ground, making his sunglasses skewwhiffed. Despite being completely out of breath, he got himself back up straightening his shades.

'Hey, what's that thing out there? asked Robin, pointing out to the sea.

Dave looked at Robin in disbelief. 'Don't you know what an oil rig is boy?' he asked.

'Oh, so that's an oil rig,' said Robin.

'What are they teaching you in school nowadays?' Dave asked in astonishment.

'Hey, there's a dog that looks a lot like Jessy over there,' said Robin ignoring the question.

'Oh right, who's Jessy?' asked Dave.

'She's Robin's friend's Dog,' explained Joan.

'Yeah, a Grey-bearded Collie-hound,' said Robin.

'That's a Border Collie, you silly swine,' said Dave.

Joan laughed, 'You've got mixed up with Lucas's other Dog, Speedy,' she said.

'Oh, right, I guess the other one is a greyhound then?' said Dave sarcastically.

'How could you know that?' asked Robin in amazement.

'Oh, the mind boggles,' said Dave as he rolled his eyes.

'I think it's about time we head back to the caravan?' he suggested.

Robin agreed, saying.

'Yeah, we should go back and watch TV.'

'What! You've not come all this way just to watch Television,' said Dave.

Robin and his family started to walk back. 'I wish I had brought my bike,' he said, looking down at the ground.

'Never mind that there's plenty of other stuff you can do while you're here,' said Dave.

'Yeah, Like what?'

Dave gave an unimpressed look towards Robin.

'Oh, the youth of today! Look, you've got the amusement arcade just over there,' explained Dave, pointing to his Left.

'And you've got the swimming pool over there,' pointing to the Right, 'What more do you need?' he asked.

Robin agreed, 'That's true, I am grateful, I just thought riding my bike around would have been fun as well.'

Dave unlocked the caravan door once they were back and opened the windows.

'Right then, let's have a nice cup of Rosy Lee,' said Dave.

'Oh yes,' said Joan as she was taking her shoes off.

Dave sat down and picked up his boating magazine, 'You can make me and your mum a cup of tea boy,' he said.

Robin huffed at the thought of the chore.

'Come on stick that stinging nettle on then,' insisted Dave.

'Oh, this kettle's taking ages man!' complained Robin impatiently.

'Well, it would do wouldn't it,' said Dave. 'You're not at home now, you've got to be careful with how much power you use in a caravan.'

'Why?' asked Robin.

'Because you'll blow the flaming fuse box,' said Dave.

'No, I mean, why can't you have as much power in a caravan?'

'Because it's not a house, it doesn't need as much.'

'Yes, it does, just look at this kettle.'

'Oh, stop whingeing. Look it's boiling now.'

Robin picked up three cups out of the cupboard taking one for himself. He put a tea bag in each cup and added the boiled water, then added milk. He passed Joan and Dave their cup of tea which was sugar-free. Robin sat down and took a sip of his own.

'Oh, no way man!' he shouted.

'What's up with you now boy?' asked Dave.

'Mine tastes salty,' said Robin.

'Which sachet did you use?'

Robin showed the empty sachet to Dave.

'I used this one,' he said.

'That's salt, you silly little swine, no bleeding wonder. I don't know, you'll spoil a good'un. Pour it down the sink and make yourself another.'

Dave shook his head, put his feet up and carried on reading his magazine. Robin's sister Jane asked if she and Lucy could go to the play area.

'Yeah, Robin can take you,' said Joan. But Robin protested, 'I'm too old to go in there now,' he said.

'I'm going to secondary school after the holidays remember.'

'Ah, rubbish, go and take them when you've drunk your tea,' said Dave.

'I don't want to,' Sneered Robin.

'Go on, take your sister and cousin, there's a splendid little Chap.' Robin looked embarrassed.

'Go on- Go on- Go on boy,' said Dave teasingly.

'Don't want to,' said Robin.

'Oi, you'll have Sydney the slipper in a minute.'

Robin swigged his tea, 'I'm bored now,' he said.

'Well, go and take them to the play area like we've been asking for the last half hour,' said Dave.

'Fine!' said Robin. 'I will.'

He put on his shoes, and when Jane and Lucy were ready, he took them to the play park. Once they had entered the gate, Jane and Lucy ran over to the slide. To keep a close eye on them he decided to watch from one of two swings and sat on the one to the Right.

The girl who he'd seen riding her bike earlier was in there too with her little brother. She noticed Robin sitting there alone and came over to him and sat on the other swing to his Right. Robin sat there quietly.

 'Hello,' she said.

Robin turned to her,

'Hello,' he replied.

She smiled at him, 'What's your name?' she asked.

 'Er, Robin,' he answered nervously.

She giggled, 'I'm Laura, what's your name?'

'It's Robin,' he said, 'I've seen you cycle on your bike by my caravan.'

'You have? Where is it?' asked Laura.

 'Is that it over there by the slide?' asked Robin.

Laura laughed, 'I meant your caravan,' she said.

'Oh, it's F twenty-one,' answered Robin.

'That's near mine, which is E-five. I thought I'd seen you,' said Laura.

'Really?' asked Robin as the feeling from adrenalin took hold of his body.

'Yeah, I've seen you when you've been sitting on the caravan step,' she said. 'Where are you from?' she asked.

'Don't worry, I'm not trying to chat you up or anything.'

Robin smiled, 'I'm from Dudley,' he said.

'Oh right. Where's that?' she asked.

'Near Wolverhampton, how about you? Where are you from?' he asked.

'Halstead,' said Laura as she held eye contact with Robin.

'Cool, where's that?' he asked.

'Essex, it's about two hours away from here, would you like to ride my bike?'

'No, thanks anyway.'

The two of them sat there for a short while, with Laura not taking her eyes off Robin as he sat quietly.

'I've got to take my brother back now,' she said, 'Maybe see you tomorrow?'

'Yes,' said Robin.

'Cool, I'll see you tomorrow,' she said.

Robin watched as Laura walked out of the gate with her brother, she waved at him with a big smile as she left. The sun was setting, and the air began to cool, the summer sun began to disappear. Robin called his sister and cousin.

'Time to get back now, come on.' Robin got out of the seat of the swing and fell to the ground. Eventually, the feeling came back in his legs and the three of them walked back to their caravan.

'Have a good time?' asked Dave.

'Yeah, it wasn't bad,' said Robin hiding the fact that he couldn't wait to see Laura again.

'Good lad, see it wasn't much trouble taking them, was it?

Now, how about you have a shower before bed?'

'Oh no, not a shower,' complained Robin.'

'Ooh, you dirty sod, just think about all the sweat and sand. Manners make a man, early to bed, early to rise, makes a young man healthy, wealthy and wise.'

Robin wondered, 'I haven't heard that saying before,' he said. Dave got up to make a cup of tea.

'Yes, boy, you'll learn a lot if you do as you're told.

'Hey Dave, can I borrow your boat magazine to read in bed tonight?'

'If you get a wash first, then yes.'

'Yes! Thanks, Dave,' said Robin as he rushed for a shower, he washed quickly to get a look at the magazine. He wished his family goodnight and got into bed. Robin woke up the next morning to find he had squashed the boat magazine.

'Oh no, Dave's going to flip,' he thought.

Robin tried to get the magazine straightened out the best he could. He heard Laura on her bike pass by, he peeked through the curtains to see her, but she had already passed before he had a chance to see her properly. Robin got dressed and he and his family had breakfast.

'You don't need all that sugar on your cereal boy,' cried Dave.

'And don't get another glass out, look at all these you've already used.' After breakfast, Dave washed up and took Robin, Jane, Lucy and Joan to the local seaside town in the car. They went to the rocky beach, and Robin threw a pebble at one of the rocks, which ricocheted back towards Dave, hitting him in the thigh.

'Oh-A! You crazy nutcase, are you mad? I'll boot your backside to Texas and back!'

Robin was embarrassed.

'Sorry!' he said worriedly. Dave rubbed his thigh and shook his head while Joan smothered her laughter. Why is it holidays are nothing like the adverts? Shouted an angry Dave.

Chapter 6
FUN AND GAMES

In the entertainment complex, Robin was enjoying a dandelion and burdock while playing cards with Dave, Joan was content just tapping her foot to the music while Jane and Lucy were with the other little children over on the dance floor.

'You can't play that card, you silly little turp, said Dave,' 'How many times do I need to go through the rules you silly sod?' he said.

Laura came in with her family, and Robin noticed her at once.

Smash! The dandelion and burdock had gone all over Dave and his playing cards.

Dave jumped from his seat, 'What's got into you,' he asked, 'Wasp in your pants or something?' Robin was sat there feeling like a fool. 'What's this music?' asked Joan.

'It's *"Higher State of Consciousness"* by Josh Wink,' replied Robin.

'Yeah right! Said Dave, 'I've got a heightened state of consciousness now.' He then headed back to the caravan to change his jeans. Laura saw Robin sitting there, staring at the stage, he looked over at her and they locked eyes, she smiled at him and waved.

Robin shyly smiled and waved back; he saw her say something to her dad. She walked over to Robin and asked, 'Would you like to go to the arcade with me?

'Yeah, all right.' He got up out of his seat and the two of them left for the arcade.

Dave returned with a fresh drink for Robin.

'Where has that plank gone now?' he asked.

Joan explained that a girl had come over and they'd both gone to the arcade together. Dave rubbed his hands together. 'Right, so he's got himself a bird now, has he?'

Robin and Laura played pool together, the pool table's surface was uneven, but Robin didn't even notice until Laura mentioned it.

He was much too interested in her to concentrate on the game anyway.

'Yeah, someone's gid this table a good'un ay they,' said Robin.

'What?' Laura chuckled, 'In English this time,' she said.

'You know, gave it a hammering,' said Robin as he was taking his aim.

'You are funny, aren't you?' she said stood waiting for him to take his shot.

'Yeah, he's hilarious, ain't ya boy?' replied Dave as he crept beside Robin.

'Here's your drink boy,' he said.

Dave gave Robin an orange aid.

'Thanks, Dave.'

'And here you are me dear,' and he gave Laura one too.

Dave left them alone to continue playing.

'Why do you call your dad Dave?' asked Laura.

'He's not my dad, he's, my uncle.'

Robin chalked his cue, 'Oh, where is your dad?' She asked.

'He's not here, he couldn't get the time off work.'

Laura frowned. 'Oh, that's too bad, I think your uncle looks like Lovejoy,' she said.

"Saturday Night" by Whigfield was playing from the main show bar. This was a night to remember. Neither of them had any fifty pence pieces left for the pool table between them. Laura's parents came over.

'Hello, Robin,' said her mom as she greeted them.

'Hi,' Robin replied.

'Time to get back to the caravan now, are you ready Laura?' asked Laura's mom.

'You can see Robin tomorrow,' said her dad.

'Blimey,' thought Robin.

'Yeah, okay, see you tomorrow then Robin,' said Laura; she smiled as she left with her parents.

Robin picked his drink up from the pool table and took it back to the show bar. He joined his family and sat at the table listening to the music playing, listening to it while thinking about how much he fancied Laura. This caused Robin to have a sense of excitement he had not felt before. Along with that combined with the holiday vibe made him think his head was going to explode.

'Are you all right boy?' asked Dave.

The following morning, Dave told everyone to get ready because he was taking them out for the day.

'Ingoldmells? Where's that?' asked Robin as he handed the brochure back to Dave.

'It's over Skegness,' said Dave.

'How far is that?' asked Robin,

Dave showed Robin his map book,

'There it is, it's about two hours away,' he said. Robin thought,

'Well, that's two hours there and two hours back, so that's four hours plus the time we're there for. That's the whole day! How am I going to see Laura now?' Robin looked disappointed,

'What's wrong boy?' asked Dave.

'Nothing, what's there?' asked Robin.

'You'll see,' said Dave while getting his shoes on.

. Back on the road, they drove passed the roller-coaster Robin and Dave had been on earlier.

After a long drive, they arrived at Fantasy Island, the place where memories are made for a lifetime, according to the brochure, which had a cheeky-looking kid who looked like a greedy little git eating candyfloss, a doughnut, and an ice cream on the front. They queued for an hour to get into the park, enduring the screams of excited children and the smell of fried food. But Robin was already feeling sorry for himself being dragged on this trip. 'That's another hour added on to the day I hadn't accounted for!' He hated waiting at the best of times, he also hated big crowds.

He especially hated the teacups, but Dave insisted that he took Jane and Lucy on them and that it was harmless and would be fun. Robin disagreed. Once the chain came across, he felt his stomach churn as the cups began to spin faster and faster, while Dave giggled and waved at them. He gripped on tight with a fearful expression held on his face. He tried to close his eyes and think of something else, but it was no use, it only made him worse. He felt a surge of dizziness and nausea. He wished he could get off. It seemed like a lifetime before the ride came to an end.

He got off the ride, feeling sick and miserable. 'That will be a memory for a lifetime,' he thought. He glared at Dave, who was now in stitches as Robin couldn't walk in a straight line.

Dave suggested that they go on the log flume next. He said it would be fun and refreshing, and that it would help Robin feel better. Robin protested, saying that he was already feeling bad enough, but Dave ignored him. He dragged him along with Jane, Lucy and Joan, who seemed to have no sympathy for Robin.

The log flume was worse than the teacups. Robin hated water rides. He hated getting wet. He hated splashes. He especially hated the big drop at the end of the ride, where the log plunged into a pool of water and created a huge wave that soaked everyone in the log and everyone watching from the bridge.

He got off the ride, dripping wet and miserable. He glared again at Dave, who looked cheerful and chatty. He also glared again at Jane, Lucy and Joan, who looked amused and entertained. They had enjoyed the log flume, saying that it was cool and fun. Robin wished he had skipped it.

Dave, who was still having the time of his life and had forgotten Robin's suffering, suggested that they go on the rollercoaster next. He said it would be thrilling, and that it would help Robin dry out. Robin refused, saying that he had enough of rides for one day, but Dave ignored him, and yet again dragged him along for the ride.

The rollercoaster was the worst of all. Robin hated rollercoasters, he hated heights and most of all he hated speed. He especially hated the loops and twists and turns that made him feel like he was going to fall out of his seat and fly into the next field. He screamed like a baby as he felt the wind whip his hair and face, and the g-force press his chest. Again, he couldn't wait for it to be over.

He got off the ride, pale and shaky. He didn't glare at anyone this time, because he had no energy left. He just wanted to go home. He hoped that was the end of his misery, and this time, he was right.

The park was closing, and it was time to leave. Robin, Dave, Jane, Lucy and Joan got in the car after a long walk through all of the car parks. Robin sat in the front passenger seat, silent and sulking, while Jane, Lucy and Joan sat quietly in the back. On route, they were approaching the dreaded rollercoaster.

'How fast would you say that ride is?' asked Joan.

'It was as fast as this,' said Robin, watching it as they passed.

'Don't be daft boy!' said Dave, 'It wasn't this fast!'

'It was!' argued Robin.

'How could it be going this fast? we're travelling at forty miles per hour.'

'Well, it was. Look: *Wow*! How fast is that kid going?' said Robin.

Robin was asked to take his sister and cousin to the play park when they returned from Ingoldmells. But when they entered the playpark Robin was too late, he had missed Laura. He was ticked off for going to Ingoldmells, and when back at the caravan decided to go to his room to read The Armageddon stratagem.

It was the next morning and Robin appeared from his room. Joan asked Robin to take the girls to the park. He rushed his breakfast hoping he would have another opportunity to see Laura again. The smoke alarm was blaring again. Robin headed for the door to escape the wretched noise. Laura rode by on her bike, Robin tripped and almost fell down the steps when he saw her. She turned back looking over her shoulder and smiled at him not realising he nearly broke his neck. 'That was close,' he thought as he gripped the handrail. She propped her bike against the lamppost, which was just outside her caravan, and then she went inside. Dave silenced the alarm with the faithful dishcloth. Robin hoped that Laura would soon come out again and his heart was pounding in apprehension. But it wasn't much longer before she came back out with her brother and sister. She began to walk with them trying not to look at him again, and before they reached the next junction she turned to see if Robin was paying attention to her. He was still standing there, he smiled, and she smiled back, a little cheekier this time as she guided her siblings around the corner, which was in the direction of the playground. Robin moved inside. 'Right, you two, I'll take you to the park,' he said hoping they would jump at the chance, and Dave couldn't believe it. Jane and Lucy were watching TV and *"The Epic Crystal Craze"* was just starting.

'Okay come on now, I'm taking you over to the park,' said Robin impatiently.

'Give them a minute! They've just had breakfast,' said Joan. *"Crystal Craze"* is on anyway. You like that.'

Robin acted like he was bursting to wee.

'No, Mom, there's no time!' he said in frustration.

Joan looked at him as if he'd just landed on the planet.

'Well, I can't believe you're that desperate to take them this time,' she said.

'Yeah,' added Dave. 'It's his bird,' he said. 'He must have seen her going there.'

'No!' said Robin knowing Dave was right.

'Right, you two go with Robin so he can play with his new bird.'

Lucy and Jane sniggered amongst themselves while watching Robin get further frustrated.

'She's not my bird Dave!' he cried.

'Yeah, okay,' said Dave, 'Pull the other sausage,' he said while giving a silly wave and grinning with his eyes tight shut to wind him up even more.

Finally, Lucy and Jane got ready for the play park and left the caravan with Robin. His sister and cousin ran through the gate towards the climbing frame. Robin walked over to the swings, as he was also scouting for Laura. It was so busy in there he couldn't see her. He sat on the one swing, grabbed the chains, leaned back and gazed into the sky. He watched the clouds drift inland. He was imagining his favourite songs while thinking about Laura.

'Hi,' she said.

Robin sat back up and was surprised to see her staring back at him. She stood there in front of him. He was pleased to see her, and his heart began to thump in his chest. She was with her younger brother. She knelt at his level and whispered something into his ear while looking at Robin.

'*Go on,*' she said as she pushed her brother towards Robin. The boy muttered something, but you couldn't quite make out what he said.

Robin looked at Laura confused. She said again.

'*Go on*, tell him.'

The poor boy didn't know what he was supposed to do.

Laura persuasively nudged him, and he managed to say, 'My Sister wants.' then paused, looked back at her and she told him to forget it, and in a strop shoved him away. There was nothing else he could do, so he left the two of them alone.

Robin knew what she was insinuating but enjoyed waiting to hear her ask him out and played dumb.

'What was it you wanted your brother to ask me?'

Laura smiled shyly at him, With both hands behind her back.

'Will you go out with me?' she asked as she twisted her shoe into the dry ground.

This caused a surge of adrenaline to hit Robin in his chest.

He went on to explain. 'I've fancied you from the first time I saw you, but I haven't asked you out, because you said the other day that you weren't chatting me up, which made me think you weren't interested in me as boyfriend material.'

'Oh, I hoped that you were going to ask me instead. So that's why you haven't.'

'Oh,' said Robin.

'So, will you go out with me?'

'Yes, I'll go out with you,' he said.

Laura's eyes sparkled as she smiled, 'Now you ask me,' she said.

'Huh?' said Robin.

'Go on, you ask me now. I want to hear you ask me.'

Robin thought it a strange request but was delighted to have her full attention.

'Will you go out with me?' he asked, giving in to her need.

'Oh, yes!' she said. She grabbed his hands jumping up and down pulling his swing all over the place and wobbling him everywhere.

'Do you like that song *"MMMbop"* by Hanson? she asked.

Robin nodded, 'Oh yeah! I love it,' he said.

'Oh, Me too,' and began to sing it. Robin joined in with her, 'Let's see who can swing the highest,' she said.

'Okay, you're on!' He swung so hard in excitement from having Laura as his girlfriend. Showing off he flew out of his seat flying in the air and falling to the dusty hard ground. Thud!

'Oh, are you all right?'

Robin's face turned red. He'd not only ripped his jeans but was bleeding from the knee.

'Yep, I'm fine,' he said and made out like nothing happened.

'Oh, you're bleeding,' said Laura.

She reached down and took Robin's hand.

'There's a tap just there, we can get that cleaned up.'

Laura pulled him up from the ground and they both headed over to it.

'Put your leg on here,' she said.

Robin took off his shoe, then his sock. He balanced his foot on the stopcock taking hold of the picket fence. Laura crouched and rolled his trouser leg up; she turned on the tap slowly and rinsed his knee with both hands. Robin watched her, she looked up into his eyes and began softly cleaning his leg washing the blood and dirt away while smiling at him.

Robin remembered what his cousin Andy had said about being yourself, and he was right.

He saw other lads who were nearby who, to Robin seemed cooler. Still, they didn't seem to exist as far as Laura was concerned. When she had finished cleaning his leg she got back up and gave him a gentle tap on the shoulder. She reached for the tap and splashed him before turning it off. He picked up an empty jug that was lying next to it, as he filled it, she asked; 'What are you doing with that?' Robin raised

it as if to throw it, she laughed and tried to run, but Robin launched it at her anyway. She screamed, she was soaked, dripping wet. The two of them looked at each other for a moment, Laura looked straight into Robin's eyes and smiled.

'I fancy you,' she said, as drips of water fell to the ground from her hair and face.

Robin thought to himself, 'I can't believe that I've met someone I fancy who likes me.'

It didn't take long for the warm breeze to dry Robin's leg. 'At least you're dry now,' she said. She pulled the leg of his jeans back down. 'There you are,' she said, and Robin kissed her on the cheek.

'I should take my brother and sister back, and get myself dried now that you've soaked me,' she said. Then a thought popped into her head, so she went on to ask. 'Shall we hang out for a while after? maybe go for a walk?'

Robin was overjoyed, he realised that he finally and unexpectedly had, what Lucas and Lauren had together. He stood still thinking about exactly that when suddenly Laura poked him in the side. 'Hey! Where have you gone?' she asked.

'What do you mean?'

Laura laughed, 'You went into a trance then,' she said.

'Did I?' he said as he seemed to be dazed.

'Yes, you were, so *do you want to go for that walk?*'

'I did? I mean I do.'

A cool dude walked by around the outside of the perimeter fence with a boombox or master blaster, and *"Tongue Tied"* by Howard Goodall was playing on it.

Laura laughed and gazed at Robin's fringe. 'Come on handsome,' she said, 'Let's take our families home and go for that walk then.'

They both walked back together with their siblings. Laura noticed that her brother's shoelace had come undone, and she stopped to tie it. Meanwhile, Lucy and Jane were whispering something amongst themselves, Robin looked at them infuriatingly, knowing that they were whispering something about him and Laura. When they arrived at Laura's caravan, Laura took her siblings inside. Robin could see her mother knitting something as he watched through the open door. She looked happy and content as she sat in her chair. Robin couldn't make out what she was knitting but was intrigued by the pattern of colours that were, Red, Mustard, dark green and purple.

When Laura came back outside, Robin asked her what her mom was knitting.

'Oh, it's a scarf for my dad,' she replied.

'But it's summer,' said Robin as he was mystified.

'Yes, I know,' she said, 'It's for winter and she loves to knit, it keeps her happy.'

It was just moments later that Robin, Jane and Lucy reached the caravan where he and his family were staying. Dave was smoking a cigarette outside and greeted Robin and Laura while Jane and Lucy rushed inside to squabble over the TV.

'Oh, here you are,' he said with a grin on his face. Then he stubbed his cigarette out quickly.

'You don't have to come back yet,' he said, 'You can stay out longer if you want to.'

Robin was surprised at this, 'Dave? Been generous with how I spend my time now?' he thought. Then there was an awkward silence.

'Has He told you he plays the piano?' asked Dave.

'You never said you can play the piano,' said Laura. Robin wasn't the kind to brag. 'No, I'm not that good,' he said.

'Yes, you are,' said Dave, 'What a shame there's no keyboard here, we could have heard you play some-thing.'

Robin looked at Laura, 'Let's go for that walk then since I can't play you anything,' he said being big-headed.

'Hang on,' said Dave, 'And don't come cocky! Here, have this.' Dave gave Robin a brand new 1997 two-pound coin. 'What's this for?' asked Robin.

'Get an Ice cream or spend it in the amusements.' Robin examined it. 'I've never seen one of these before,' he said.

Laura looked over Robin's shoulder and rested her chin on it. 'No, me neither,' she said.

'Thanks, Dave,' said Robin gratefully.

Laura took Robin by the hand as they walked away. They walked along the road, passing all the other caravans, *"Fall at Your Feet"* by Crowded House was heard playing from someone's radio. Robin and Laura reached the amusement arcade. Conveniently, the pool table was unoccupied, and Laura insisted they had a game. Robin looked at the two-pound coin Dave had given him. Robin was sad to have to change it for fifty pence pieces but was delighted when they played pool together. It was a leisurely affair full of smiles and laughs, there was without a single competitive edge between them. The arcade was small, and the pool table occupied the centre. Three pinball machines had a theme of nineteen eighties science fiction which lined the back wall.

Music began playing that was *"Wipe Out"* by The Surfaris. Robin Laughed, 'That crazy laugh at the start gets me every time,' he said.

Then *"Coco Jamboo"* by Mr President came on; this was the first time Robin had heard this song and he loved it. Robin potted the black. 'Ha, wipeout!'

'You just lost silly.'

'Blast! Hey, I have an idea,' he said. 'What if we save the rest of the money for an ice cream and take it to the beach?' Laura put her pool cue down on the table.

'Yes, let's do that,' she said, her face lit up with enthusiasm. Robin left his cue next to hers on the pool table, and they both left the arcade together.

They walked to the entrance of the beach, which is where the ice cream hut was situated. The song *"When"*, by the Kalin Twins, was playing from it. They both had a ninety-nine with a flake. Robin and Laura walked onto the beach; the sun gleamed from the sea. Laura was smart and had her sunglasses with her. She laughed at Robin squinting and offered them to him, but he couldn't let her do that and refused. They walked as far as the next beach bar; *"All Right"* by Supergrass was blasting from the outdoor speakers.

Both Robin and Laura sang along to the lyrics, laughing and being silly running about on the shore and dodging the waves, trying not to lose their ice cream. She swabbed hers on his nose, and Robin laughed then rubbed it off. Then he grabbed her, gripping her tightly and acted like he was going to push her into the sea, she squealed and laughed. She began to walk, 'Come with me,' she said.

Robin followed, 'Where are you taking me?' he asked.

'You'll see.' They headed back towards the caravan park, and just before the caravan park was a path that ran along a brook. Laura found a secluded spot and sat on the grass; Robin sat opposite her there under the trees, and neither of them said a word.

Robin looked up through the trees to the blue sky, then looked back down to find Laura smiling at him. 'What are you thinking about? You crazy banana,' she asked. He pulled a handful of grass and threw it over her. She too pulled a chunk and threw it over him. He went to grab another from behind him, but she lunged forward and grabbed his arms. The next thing he knew was that they were full-on kissing each other.

His heart was beating so fast, he felt as though he was going to float off. He had never kissed a girl before. When Laura had stopped, she playfully pushed him backwards with him toppling on his back. She got up and put her hand out, smiled and said, 'Come here.' She helped him back up and cuddled him. 'You're Lovely,' she said.

They both approached the site via a gate which gave access to other private caravans. Laura was just about to open it when an old lady shouted, 'Oh no, you don't. Use the main entrance, this is private. They both ran off and went the long way around. They entered the main entrance where Laura spotted Dave, Joan, Jane and Lucy playing mini golf together.

'That's your uncle, isn't it?' she said.

'Where?' asked Robin.

'Over there, playing crazy golf with your family,' she said.

Robin and Laura walked over to them, Dave saw them coming and straightened up from trying to take his shot.

'Hey, it's Rob and his bird.'

'Don't call her that Dave,' said Robin, and Laura chuckled.

'We may as well have another game of pool since these are playing crazy golf,' Suggested Robin. Laura agreed and the two of them headed for the arcade. By the time they got there, Robin realised he was out of money for the pool table and rummaged through his pocket not realising he had another two-pound coin in the other.

'Here, I've got fifty pence,' said Laura. 'You've spent enough today, it's only fair,' she said putting it in the coin slot.

Robin set the pool balls up and let Laura have the first shot. A boy was sitting on a stool next to one of the pinball machines who was watching Laura. Robin noticed and felt at once jealous.

The boy walked over, '*Hi Laura,*' he said cheekily.

'Oh, what do you want Daniel?' she asked him.

'Oh nothing, 'he muttered. 'I was wondering if you'll be at the disco tonight?'

'I will be there, yes, but not with you!' she said sharply. 'I'm with Robin.' But Daniel didn't seem to accept this.

'What? Him?' he said, and poked Robin's nose.

'Leave us alone Dan, I told you last season I wasn't interested, so get lost.' Robin looked like he was about to explode. 'Yeah! spack off! Before I shove this cue up your.'

'No Robin!' interrupted Laura, 'Let's leave him. Enjoy the free pool creep,' she said throwing her cue down on the table.

Robin and Laura walked away with Robin following. The man in the kiosk shook his head 'Stupid Kids,' he said.

'You wouldn't have smacked him, would you?' asked Laura.

Robin smiled, 'No, I'm not like that, I hate bullies and fighting,' he said.

Laura smiled, 'I'm glad you're not a loser like that. You're one of the good ones, aren't you?'

'Yes,' replied Robin. 'My Uncle says, I'd spoil a good'un.

Laura began to laugh.

'What's so funny?' he asked.

'You, telling Dan to spack off,' she said.

'Oh Yeah I couldn't decide to say sod off or back off, and it came out like that.'

Laura laughed again, 'Let's go back to mine,' she said, 'We can sit outside and play cards.'

'Okay, sounds good to me,' said Robin reaching for her hand.

They walked hand in hand together as they walked towards her caravan. Someone had their caravan door open along the way, and "Countdown" with Carol Vorderman and Richard Whiteley, was on their TV.

Laura tugged Robin, 'Why are we stopping?' she asked.

'I think I can make a word from that,' he said.

'From what?'

'From Countdown on that TV,' he said.

'Ooh that's naughty, you shouldn't be looking inside other people's caravans like that,' said Laura as they continued to walk.

'So, what word did you come up with?' she asked.

He replied with, "Chicken check."

'What? chicken shed?'

'No, Chicken check.'

'Chicken neck?'

'*No,* Chic, -hen, -check,'

'Oh, but that's three words,' said Laura.

'No, it's not, it's Chickencheck,'

'No, I don't think so, you can't have chicken check as a word,' said Laura laughing. 'Stuff the cards, I'll challenge you to Scrabble,' she vowed.

When they got to her caravan, her mother Maureen, was sitting outside continuing her knitting, and her dad was sitting in his chair listening to the radio.

Laura went inside to get Scrabble. 'Oh, Hi Robin, how are you doing?' asked her dad Geoff. 'I'm fine thanks.'

'Here, get yourself a chair mate,' he said.

Laura came back with Scrabble, 'I thought we could play this,' she said, 'As Robin needs to learn.'

She set up the game on the table and Geoff got up and poured them all a cloudy lemonade each from the jug, passing one to Maureen first.

'Why does Robin need to learn?' asked Geoff, 'Has he not played Scrabble before?'

'No, but I can play countdown,' replied Robin.

Laura's mother looked at Laura and then at Robin, 'Well, I suppose it is similar, so you'll be fine Robin,' she said.

'No, he needs to learn, saying things like chicken check,' said Laura.

Geoff spat out his lemonade and laughed,

'What's a chicken check when it's at home?' he asked.

'A coop,' said Maureen.

Laura's parents left Robin and Laura to play Scrabble together.

'You can't have that, you crazy banana,' said Laura.

'Forget chicken check, I'll say flipping heck,' said Robin frustratedly.

'What's he put? Asked Maureen.'

'He's gone and put, Kittiwake.'

'Kittiwake ay?' said Geoff.

'Yes, he can have that,' said Maureen. 'It's a Gull.'

'A seagull, a seagull' Robin sang as he danced like a chicken.

Robin's family came over on their way back from playing mini golf, and Robin was still dancing like a chicken. 'Ah, here you are Boy,' said Dave, 'Have you finally gone mad?'

"I'm going slightly mad" by Queen came on Geoff's Radio and everyone began to laugh except for Robin.

'Right, just to let you know that I've decided to do a Barbie later,' said Dave, 'You can bring Laura along too.

'Oh, yes!' said Robin, 'Would you like to?' he asked; giving Laura puppy eyes. 'What a friendly gesture, you go if you want to Laura,' suggested Maureen.

'Yes, okay I would love that.' Said Laura.

'Splendid,' said Dave, 'We'll see both of you love birds later.'

Robin and Laura continued to play Scrabble. Laura smiled and added an 'L' to the end of 'ZOO,' making 'ZOOLOGY' and scoring nineteen points. 'Oh, nickers!' Robin frowned and looked at his tiles. He had a Q, a U, an X, an E, an R, a T and an A. He scanned the board for a place to put his Q, but there was none. He sighed and exchanged his Q for another tile, losing his turn.

Laura grinned and placed the word 'QUIZ' on the board, using the Z from 'ZOOLOGY' and scoring twenty-two points. She winked at Robin and said, 'Sorry, I couldn't resist.' Robin rolled his eyes and looked at his new tile. It was another Q. He groaned 'Oh flipping heck,' he said and threw his tiles on the table. Laura laughed and said, 'Don't worry, maybe you'll get lucky next time.'

She reached for her tiles and picked one up. It was a Q. She gasped and looked at Robin with disbelief. He burst out laughing and said, 'Now that's karma for you.' They both laughed and continued to play until the smell of Dave's barbecue wafted over.

'Maybe we should go to the barbecue now, 'suggested Laura, 'we don't want to keep Dave waiting after all.'

'Yeah, that smells good, doesn't it?' said Robin, taking a sniff of the air.

Laura began to pack away the game pieces back in its box.

Meanwhile, Dave is losing his rag after dropping the second sausage on the ground from trying to turn it over. He then stamped on it in a fit of rage, 'There! you want to be on the ground, so get in the ground, you fat git!

'Who's a fat git?' Asked Robin as he and Laura walked over; 'And what is that by your foot? Oh no! You've stepped in a dog egg Dave,' he said.

Laura looked disgusted and held her nose.

'It's not dog muck, it's a sausage,' said Dave sharply.

Robin looked confused while Laura looked amused.

'Why is it squashed then?' asked Robin.

'Never mind that dear boy, pass me a lager from the fridge, would you? Robinson.'

Joan came out of the caravan and gave him one anyway. 'Thanks, Vic,' he said.

'I thought you said your mom's name was Joan?' asked Laura.

Robin laughed, 'It is, he just calls her that because he thinks she looks like the vicar of Dibley.'

Laura didn't seem impressed.

'Oh, that's cheeky of him,' she said.

Dave was working so hard over the hot grill his face was dripping with sweat. A bead of sweat dripped from Dave's nose into the barbeque and with a hiss, it hit the hot coals.

'Ugh,' gasped Robin.

'What's up with you boy?' asked Dave defensively.

'*Nothing,*' replied Robin.

'So why do you look like a bulldog chewing a wasp?'

Laura Laughed. 'Don't encourage him,' said Robin.

'Ok, *Robinson,*' she said teasingly.

'Oh no,' said Robin, 'Not you too.'

Chapter 7
TAKE THE PLUNGE

Robin found himself in a clinical type of laboratory. He felt someone grab his shoulder from behind and whisper, 'Run from this place, he is coming.' Robin was so scared he was frozen with fear. He turned around expecting someone to be there, but nothing except a small, strange object on a hospital bed. It was made up of wires, mechanical, and organic matter.

'Oh, my life it's a brain,' he thought. The brain screamed in a robotic-sounding voice from its vocoder, 'Run! Get out of here before you become like us.' Robin tried to run, but he was not going anywhere. He had his eyes set on the two double

134

doors on the other side of the room but only moved forward two inches. He looked down at his feet and they were running, but he was stuck on the spot. He then felt like he was being pulled backwards and turned his head towards the conscious brain. It desperately shouted 'Go! Now!' Robin slowly forced himself out of the room. In slow motion, he ran to a lift that had the feel of a 1950s elevator, fell inside of it and landed in the back corner. The lift began to react like it was out of control, speeding downwards. It finally came to a halt, and the doors opened at once. Something terrifying was entering from the darkness, Robin was kicking and yelling, '*NO "Bungamungoo"*, NO!'

There was a huge hammering sound coming from the right. It sounded like someone thumping hard on a thin cardboard wall, and then a loud voice shouted,

'What the heck are you bleeding doing, you silly swine? It's three o'clock in the blasted morning. Keep the noise down in there.'

Robin was awakened by Dave's angry shouting and found himself in a sweat entangled in his bed sheets on the floor. He got back onto the bed and eventually fell asleep.

'*They're coming to take me away, ha-haaa!*" by Napoleon XIV' was playing on the radio the next morning followed by, *"I'm not Scared"* by Eight Wonder.

Dave came into Robin's room with a puzzled expression on his face. 'Here, what was all that commotion in the night?' he asked. 'Were you having nightmares or what? And what's a Bungamungoo when it's at home?'

Robin was just about to explain; It's what you say when you can't get your words out when sleep talking, but Dave noticed the book first, *"The Armageddon Stratagem"* on the bedside cabinet, and said, 'No bleeding wonder boy.' He picked it up.

"The Armageddon Stratagem"

'Right! You're not reading this anymore,' he said and took the book away.

Robin guessed that Dave would hide it away along with the Trump spray he had bought from the joke shop the other day.

Laura called round for Robin and knocked on the caravan door, she was dressed for swimming.

Dave began singing "Let 'Em In" by Wings.

Joan answered the door and made Laura welcome.

Laura asked if Robin would go to the swimming pool with her and her dad. 'Yeah, let's go,' said Robin hastily.

'I think you'll need to change first,' said Joan.

'Oh yeah,' said Robin.

Laura and Robin laughed. Dave shook his head while picking up his newspaper.

Robin went to his room and got changed quickly.

'Blimey! That was quick,' said Laura.

'What car does your dad drive?' asked Dave.

'It's a Volvo,' she replied.

'Oh Yeah, we saw a Volvo estate the other day when we were going into Hunstanton, and a car went into the back of it.'

'Yeah, that was ours,' she said.

'No way. That happened to you?' asked Robin in surprise.

'It smashed the backlights didn't it,' he said.

Laura gave a little smile and quietly said, "*Yeah.*"

She glanced out of the kitchen window.

'Oh, it's my dad, come on Robin, we better meet him.'

Robin and Laura both left the caravan together. They caught up with Geoff and walked with him to the pool. The sun was beating down on this yet another hot day. *"Just Ask Your Heart"* by Frankie Avalon was playing from the outdoor speakers of the entertainment bar. You could still hear the music from inside the pool complex. Robin went to push Laura straight into the pool, and she laughed. He stood staring into her face; she smiled back and suddenly shoved him backwards. His arms swung in the air, and then in he went with a massive splash. She dived in next to him, and once she appeared from the water's surface, she smiled at him again, he smiled back and splashed her straight in the face. She then grabbed his shoulders and pulled him under the water.

'Okay, steady on you too,' shouted Geoff as he hobbled over to the edge.

'They'll be making love in a minute,' he said climbing in.

He swam up to them singing, '*Splish Splash*, by Bobby Darin.'

Robin made a foothold from his hands and told Laura to put her foot in it.

'Why?' she asked.

'Come on, trust me,' he said. 'And face the other way.'

'What for?'

'Face that way with your back to me and put your foot here.'

Robin waited with his hands locked, she put her right foot in. Robin launched her up and she flew landing back into the pool. She swam back to him and said, 'Here I'll do that to you now.'

Geoff began to laugh, 'Oh you pair,' he said.

'Here I'll send him, you'll break your back doing it.'

'Dad, he doesn't want to be launched by you.'

Robin wondered, and said, 'Go on, it'll be fun.'

And sure, enough Robin gave it a go. Geoff thrust him up like a rocket. He flew up four times more than what Laura had.

'*Ah*, Dad! That's too hard.'

But it was too late. Geoff looked worried, 'He's all right, look,' he said.

Robin landed flat on the water's surface on his stomach. Now Underwater, his eyes were a squint and air bubbles blew from his mouth as he screamed out "*Ahh.*"

Laura swam over to him, 'Ooh, are you okay? You smacked the water hard, I heard it.'

'Yeah, I'm okay thanks, it came sharp though.'

'You ok old chap?' asked Geoff.

'Oh no!' gasped Laura.

'What?' asked Robin.

'It's Daniel.'

Robin sighed, 'Oh, that's just great isn't it.'

Daniel came to the pool's edge and got in.

'He's coming this way,' said Laura.

He came behind Robin, 'All right you two?' he said poking Robin in the back.

'Touch me again, and I'll drown you, you git and slap you on your sunburn,' said Robin gritting his teeth.

'Ok, now-now children.' Said Geoff.

'Just, get lost, Dan! Spack off,' said Laura.

'That's right, sod off,' Robin added.

Daniel sniggered and moved away leaving them alone.

'That was close wasn't it,' said Laura,

'Yeah, he nearly got choked like a chicken,' said Robin.

'I thought they would have to close the pool for the bloody water,' said Geoff. Well, I'm going to call it a day,' he added.

'Yeah, let's get out now,' suggested Laura. the three of them swam to the steps and climbed out. Laura turned to Robin, 'I'll meet you back outside if you like,' she said.

Robin headed back to the caravan to get dried and changed. His family were just coming out of the door when he got there.

Dave was holding a beach towel in one hand while he was about to lock up.

Ah, young Billy Bob. We were just on our way to find you,' he said.

'You weren't there long,' Joan said in surprise.

Robin pondered for a moment.

'I could go back and meet you after I'm changed,' he said. 'I said that I would meet Laura outside anyway.'

'All right, that's all set,' said Dave as he passed the key to Robin. 'We'll see you down there. Come on then, let's go,' he added as he tumbled down the steps.

'Ooh! Are you Okay?' asked Joan. Dave didn't answer, he just got himself up off the ground and dusted himself down. He, Joan and the girls left for the pool, leaving Robin to change.

Robin went to his room, closed the door behind him and burst into laughter, hoping that Dave was far enough away to hear him.

'Right, I'm going to wear my best clothes to keep Laura keen,' he thought.

He rummaged through his draw and found his favourite shorts and t-shirt. He closed the draw catching his finger in it. "*Ahh*! That serves me right for laughing at Dave doesn't it".

Once Robin was dry and changed, he walked back to the Pool complex.

Laura was already waiting and took him by the hand. 'So, what shall we do now?' she asked.

'Well, my family have gone inside, and I said we would meet them in there.'

'Oh right, ok,' she said.

They both walked back inside hand in hand to the pool but there were no spare chairs to sit on.

'Oh, this is pants,' said Robin, 'There's nowhere to sit and it's too hot in here.'

'It's ok, we can just stand and watch,' said Laura.

Dave swam up to the pool's edge, 'What are you whingeing at now Robinson dear boy?' he asked. 'Don't tell me you've lost the caravan key.'

'*No*? It's too hot Dave, it's far too hot,' said Robin wafting his top.

'Ahh, stop your whining boy.'

'No! It's so hot,' said Robin as he handed Dave the key.

'Right boy, we'll just have to cool you off won't we.'

The lifeguard was passing. 'Here mate,' said Dave. 'Would you do us all a favour and throw him in here?' he asked.

The lifeguard looked at Robin, picked him up and walked back a couple of paces. He ran straight towards the pool.

Robin thought the lifeguard was pulling a prank. Surely, he wouldn't throw him in fully clothed, would he? But the lifeguard ran forward and jumped into the air, Robin saw only water beneath him as the tiled flooring was now behind him.

Splash! The lifeguard and Robin both went in together. Laura stood still. Her hand over her mouth as Robin came up to the water's surface. He climbed out with everyone watching.

'Better now boy?' asked Dave before laughing his head off.

'No! He's wet my bloody trainers!'

Dave laughed harder, and Laura tried to hold in her laughter with a strain.

'Oh dear, better get you back to get dry again,' she said.

'All right, let's leave these sad acts here,' said Robin, 'Dave, give me the caravan key,' he demanded.

'Your mom has it,' said Dave.

Robin walked over to Joan dripping wet, she smirked and handed him the key.

Laura followed Robin out of the Pool complex. Once they arrived at his caravan, he unlocked the door, and they moved inside.

'I won't be long; I'm going to get out of these wet clothes,' he said.

'I can't believe the lifeguard put you in the pool with all your clothes on.'

'Neither can I,' said Robin, as he disappeared into the bathroom.

Laura sat in the lounge while she waited for him. She secretly found it fun, Robin being tossed into the pool like that. As for the attention it got him, so did he.

Robin came into the lounge from his room after getting changed. 'Second time you've had to get changed today isn't it,' said Laura.

Robin sat to the right side of her and said, 'Yeah, what a joke.' He put his arm around her, and she leaned the side of her face on his shoulder.

'You're so handsome,' she said.

He turned to face her, and they gazed into each other's eyes and slowly moved in for a kiss.

'You're so pretty, I'm so glad I met you,' he said and pulled her in for another. After a few moments passed they both broke it off. Robin began to comb her hair softly with his fingers and she saw a book on the table, it was *"Persuasion" by* Jane Austen. 'Who's is that book?' she asked.

'Why it's my mom's,' explained Robin. 'Do you like reading?' he asked.

'Yes, I love reading.'

  'Me too, are you reading anything at the moment?'

'Yes, *"The Secret Diary of Adrian Mole"* by Sue Townsend, what are you reading *Robinson*?' asked Laura teasingly.

'Oh no, don't call me that as well.'

Laura chuckled and poked Robin's nose. 'Well, are you reading anything at the moment?' she asked.

'Yeah. Well, that was until Dave confiscated it.'

'Why ever would he do that?'

'He thinks it gives me nightmares,' said Robin. Laura laughed,

'What?' said Laura with a massive grin on her face.

'What kind of story is it?' she asked.

'It's just some sci-fi,' said Robin.

'What's it about?'

'It's about a man who survived radioactive poisoning from a nuclear war in the future and wants to rule the planet he's from, doing all kinds of bizarre stuff to try and do it.'

'Oh, right, I'm not a big fan of science fiction, but that sounds interesting,' she said. Robin couldn't

think of anything else to say, but Laura was good at keeping a conversation going. 'So where do you think Dave hid your book?' she asked.

'I don't know, but he did well to hide it in this caravan. I guess he's hidden it away with the Trump spray.'

Laura laughed and looked at Robin in a patronising manner, 'What did you buy that for?' she asked.

'I didn't!' said Robin defensively. 'He bought that.'

Laura was intrigued. 'Oh? Why would he hide it if it was him who'd bought it?'

'Well, he sprayed it in here the other day and said, it smelt like a thousand-year-old tinned pump by a pig and had been brewed with poultry poo for one hundred and fifty years in a stink tank. Then he opened all the windows up until the stench went away.'

Laura pulled a shocked face. 'Wow, it must be pretty bad then,' she said. 'Hey, let's see if we can find your book.'

'No way! He'll go stark raving nuts.'

At that moment, Dave, Joan, Lucy and Jane came in through the door. 'Alright drip, drip-drip-drip,' said Dave. Everyone had a good laugh at Robin's ordeal, and even Robin also saw the funny side too.

Wasps began to come in through the kitchen window and Dave quickly rummaged through a drawer and pulled out what he thought was Wasp killer spray. Unfortunately, it was the Trump spray, and he gave it a good blast off, towards the wasps. His face was a picture as he jolted.

'Pour-Ya! _ *"That's a real fruity force ten!'* he yelled as

he gripped his nose. Laura pulled a disgusted face and Robin said, '**Eugh**! Let's get the flip out of here.'

Chapter 8

OUT OF TIME

Robin's dad Brien pulled up outside the caravan as Laura and Robin were on their way out when Robin greeted his dad Brien. Brien was surprised to see that Robin was with a girl and it was written on his face that he was pleased. They both walked ahead as Brien entered the caravan. They walked by the playground; they saw it was empty and sat on the swings where they had first met. The sun had almost gone down, and the air was fresh. Robin experienced a moment of disappointment, as he knew the holiday was near its end. He watched Laura as her hair gently blew in the breeze, and she said very little.

'Will we see each other again once we've left this place?' asked Robin.

Laura sighed, 'We can swap addresses and write to each other once we're home,' she said, 'We could have each other's phone numbers too and can call each other.

Robin felt uplifted by the thought, 'Yes, that would be great,' he said cheerfully.

Laura got up and said, 'Come on I'll race you to that slide,' she leapt ahead, and Robin dashed after her. They both ran so fast; the ground seemed like a blur to them. Robin caught up with her and got hold of her arms, she sighed and put her head in his chest.

'I love you, Robin,' she said in a soft voice.

'And I love you' He replied fighting for his breath. They both laughed and then hugged.

'Here they are,' said Dave as he stood at the gate with Brien.

'Hey up boy, we're going to the pub. Your mom did your packing you lazy swine, what the heck have you been up to? There's sand all over you.'

Robin took Laura's hand, 'I should go now,' he said, and Laura looked sad.

'Come with us,' Robin asked hopefully.

'I need to pack, most likely for my sister and brothers too.' I'll see if my parents will let me though,' she said.

'Let's leave them to it,' said Brien.

'We should go,' said Robin, 'And see if you can come out with us to the pub.

They walked out through the gate and had a slow walk back. Laura asked Robin to get his details written down for her and to meet at her caravan. Robin burst into his caravan like a whirlwind in haste to find a piece of paper and pen. 'Here! What's your game?' shouted Dave in shock.

'I need a piece of paper and a pen!' cried Robin.

Brien reached into his trouser pocket and pulled out the car keys and passed them to him.

'There's some paper in the glove box and pens in the centre console.'

Robin went outside to the Ford Escort, unlocked it and sat in the passenger seat.

Laura walked over; she could see the top of his head through the windscreen as he was looking down into the glovebox; her heart skipped. She walked up to the open door and tapped it twice. He looked up and smiled when he saw her. She came around the door and stood next to him and he looked up with squinted eyes. Laura knelt at his level and then handed him a note with her address and landline number on it. He looked at it for a moment then put it safely inside the car manual and began writing his note to give her.

'Oh, you're left-handed, there's always something new and interesting to find out about you isn't there?' she said.

Robin smiled and handed her the note. She read it and asked, 'Are all the roads by you named after poets?'

'Yes, they are,' He replied.

'Aw, that's romantic, I like poetry,' she said.

As he listened to Laura, Robin was aware that this amazing time with her was coming to an end and time was running out.

Dave came out of the caravan, 'Are you ready boy? We're off to the pub,' he said.

'Which one?' asked Robin as he closed the glovebox.

'The Northwest Norfolk' replied Dave.

Robin asked Laura if she could come too.

'I can't,' she said. 'I've still got to pack my sisters' case.'

Robin was heavily disappointed. He hugged her as he and his family left for the pub. They walked along the disused railway line which ran alongside the holiday park. They arrived at the pub and sat on a bench outside.

'Right, what are we all drinking?' asked Dave.

'I'll have a "Suffolk punch",' said Robin.

'That's a pony ain't it?' asked Dave.

'I thought it was a lawnmower,' said Brien.

'No, it's a blasted cider!' shouted Robin.

'Erm! You'll have a ginger Pop,' said Dave.

'I don't want a ginger pop; I want a "Suffolk punch"!' scowled Robin.

'You'll have a size ten in Norfolk punch from me in a minute if you don't behave, what would your bird think if she saw you behaving like this?'

Robin went quiet as soon as that was said.

'Dave?'

Yes, how can I help now boy?'

'Can I have a dandelion and burdock instead please?'

'That's more like it boy, if they haven't got that it's Ginger Pop.'

In the morning Robin was sat on the caravan steps. He could see that Laura and her family were about to leave. Their car was jam-packed full, and their bikes were stowed on the rack. When he saw hers, he remembered her riding it around, which to him felt like a long time ago. Brien came outside and stood with Robin. He guessed that Robin was waiting to see Laura for the last time. She was in the back of the car with her brothers and sister. Geoff started the car and began to drive slowly. Robin watched as they approached him, they were coming up to the junction which was right opposite. Laura and her family all began to wave as they got closer. Robin and Brien both waved back, Robin looked straight at Laura, and she smiled at him, still waving. They turned right, he watched them go down towards the right-hand bend; Robin could see the broken backlight from the rear. Robin saw their car slowly disappear around the corner thinking,

'That's it then.'

He stood still for a short while,

'What do I do now?' he wondered.

The whole place seemed quiet, and glum.

He began to walk in the direction Laura and her family had just left. He walked alone leaving Brien and the caravan behind hiding the pained expression on his face. He walked by the amusement arcade and saw the lonely pool table inside, he looked away and continued. He walked out of the site and along the brook. He found the place where he and Laura first kissed. He looked up through the trees as they hissed with fresh air; the sun broke through into his eyes as he stood alone. It might have been five minutes or more before he walked on again. He arrived at the beach, then paused; and listened to the chirp of swifts and the sound of the calm sea gently swishing the shore. There was a clanging of a distant flagpole, the beach bar was opening and began to play music, the music that was *"Oxygène part Six"* by Jean Michel Jarre. Robin followed the beach for a short while and came across the sand dunes. He walked through the small valleys and came across a lonely windmill, he watched as the sails turned slowly, there was a cool breeze and the windmill groaned as it worked. Robin could stand the depressing sound no longer and headed back to his caravan. He looked through the swimming pool's glass panels and stared at the closed pool along the way. He changed his mind about going back to the caravan and wanted to see the play area swings one last time, so he walked around to them. He walked up to the picket fence rested against it and sighed. The swings squeaked gently in the sea breeze, there was a thick black cloud approaching and the sun disappeared behind it. Robin stared at the two swings and shivered, then an unpleasant sensation came over him like he couldn't breathe.

'I want to go home,' he said to himself. 'No, I want Laura,' he thought.

Dave came over to him and said 'Are you alright Robinson? We were wondering where you'd got to.'

'No, I'm not all right,' said Robin.

'Come on, you'll be all right. No good retracing your steps torturing yourself like this.'

'How would you know that's what I'm doing?'

'Believe me, I've been there; I was your age once. Let's get you back, your mom and dad are waiting to go home.'

Robin nodded, 'Yes, time to leave,' he said.

Chapter 9
HOME AND DRIVE

Dave gave the book The Armageddon Stratagem back to Robin and locked the caravan door for the last time.

Robin looked down at the book in his hands, 'I don't want to read anymore,' he said.

'Of course, you do boy,' said Dave.

Robin looked at the front cover, 'My gums feel numb' he said.

'Okay "numb gum", I think you're working yourself up a bit too much now. Go on get in your dad's car there's a good chap and we'll see you again soon.'

Robin got into the car with his family. Brien started up the engine. Robin stared out the rear window as he passed all the caravans and finally came to the exit. The car turned out of the site with Dave in front. They drove up the road with a view of the caravan park below. Robin watched as the caravan site disappeared behind some wild brambles, and then it was gone. Brian followed Dave as far as Peterborough and Dave branched off for Leicester. Rain began to batter the windscreen and the sky turned black. '*Fragile, by Sting*' was playing on the radio. Robin just sat still gazing through the window feeling sorry for himself, and to make things worse, "*No more 'I Love You's,*" by Annie Lennox, played next.

After another two hours, Robin was finally home. He took his and Jane's case upstairs, he put Jane's case in her room first. There was a poster of '*Hanson,*' on her wall and the sun began to shine through the window on it. Robin noticed she had left the cassette tape '*MMMbop*' on the bed. He borrowed it and took his case to his room. He put the cassette in his tape deck, and pressed play. He closed his eyes and remembered singing it on holiday with Laura. This made him feel lightheaded and not well, so he switched to the radio and '*Same Old Scene, by Roxy Music*' was on. Not a lot happened that evening, Brien fell asleep in the armchair, Joan did all the laundry and Jane just sat in front of the TV.

The following day Lucas called,

'How was the holiday?' he asked excitedly.

Robin offloaded all that happened, and how he met Laura and that he had her phone number.

'Have you phoned her yet?' asked Lucas, inquisitively.

'No, not yet.'

'Why the devil not!'

'Well, I thought I would give her some time to settle in after the holiday.'

'No stupid, you call her now.'

'What, right now?'

'Yes, right now! She's most likely waiting for you.'

'But I thought she would call if she wasn't busy.'

'No, it doesn't work that way, if you want to show you care about her_'

'I do!'

'Well call her then.'

Robin looked at the telephone,

'*Dad*? Can I phone Laura?'

'Okay but tell her to call back if you're going to be long, I'm not made of money,' said Brien throwing his voice from the lounge.

Robin picked up the phone and dialled her number reading it from the note on top of the phone book. Laura's mother Maureen answered, so Robin asked if he could speak to Laura. Robin heard Maureen call for her and say it was Robin for her, and Maureen handed the handset to Laura.

'Hello?' she said.

'Hello, it's Robin.'

'Hi,' she said enthusiastically, 'I was hoping it was you.'

'Really?' asked Robin excitedly.

'Yes, I miss you,' she said.

Robin was pleased to be speaking with her again.

'I miss you too, I want to see you again,' he said.

'I want to see you too Robin.'

'But how? I live in the Midlands, and you live in the Essex.'

Laura laughed, 'It's just Essex,' she said. 'Yeah, I don't know; tricky isn't it,' she said in dismay.

'I should go now; my mom is calling me to do some more chores.'

'Okay, we can talk again soon,' said Robin.

'Yeah, that would be nice. Bye then Robin, love you.'

Robin looked at Lucas and back to the phone and said quietly,

'I love you too,' so as not to be heard by his mom or dad.

He put the handset back in its dock.

'See, that wasn't so bad, was it?' said Lucas.

'No, it wasn't, it was good to hear her voice again.'

Lucas looked pleased and began singing "I know you're out there somewhere," by The Moody Blues.

'Stop it, Lucas, you'll just make me sad again.'

It was the day after, and Robin called for Lucas. They visited the golf course and sat in the rough of hole four.

Facing southeast they could see for miles. Looking out over Cotwall End Valley they could see as far as Birmingham one way, and Banbury the other.

Robin wondered,

'I wonder how far Essex is from here,' he said.

Lucas looked up at a cloud which looked a similar shape to Britain.

'*Miles and miles*, oh sorry.'

'Do you think we might see it from here?' asked Robin, as he was fiddling with a daisy he had just picked.

'I wouldn't think so, I think it must be at least a thousand miles away,' said Lucas as he laid back looking up to the sky.

'When are you seeing Lauren next?' asked Robin.

'That will be when she's back from her holidays.' Lucas replied. 'I wished she was here,' he added.

Robin pulled out Brien's Air and Marine radio, he tried to tune in to an aeroplane, but Lucas said to just find Beacon Radio instead, so Robin tuned in until he found it.

'Hey, I like this, what is it?' Robin asked.

"Children by Robert Miles", said Lucas.

When they had worn the batteries down, they decided to walk on. 'I would like to call Laura again,' said Robin.

'You can use the phone box on Longfellow Road,' said Lucas. They cut across the school playing field when they noticed the bullies from school.

'Don't look at them, let's just walk quickly without them noticing us,' said Lucas.

'Hey look, it's Robin and Lucas,' said David Thomas.

'Well, if it's not Tom Grimer,' said Lucas.

'Don't let him hear you say that' said Robin worriedly.

'Come here!' shouted Mike Redford.

'Yeah,' said Tom Climber.

'Come on, let's go back,' said Robin.

'Yeah, let's move before they come over,' said Lucas.

Robin and Lucas turned back to go the long way

around. Robin heard stomping and knew it was the bullies running up to them. Lucas turned around when Smack! Straight on his nose, Tom punched him, and David wrestled Robin to the ground ripping his t-shirt.

Lucas's nose was bleeding, Robin managed to get to his feet and punched David in the stomach, sending him into the drainage ditch. Tom tried to pull him back out, but Lucas shoved them both back into it.

'Let's get out of here,' said Robin.

Lucas agreed and they both ran out to the main road.

'Are you okay?' asked Robin, bruised and grass-stained.

'Not really,' muttered Lucas.

'I'm glad Laura didn't see that happen,' said Robin.

'I'm glad Lauren didn't either,' said Lucas. 'Let's go back to mine,' he said, 'Let's get cleaned up, I have a spare top you can borrow, and you can call Laura from the phone box after.'

'Oh no' moaned Robin sadly.

'What?' asked Lucas.

'I've lost my change, it must have come out over the field, I bet those idiots have it now.'

'Oh no,' said Lucas. 'It's okay, I've got some at home,' he said.

'I'm glad my dad's radio didn't get damaged,' said Robin in relief.

They continued to walk when a man walking his dog was passing,

'What's that'? he asked,

'Oh, it's my dad's radio,' said Robin.

'Hey, you better be careful, you can pick up the police on that, you know.'

'Can you?' asked Lucas.

'I don't know,' said Robin.

The man offered to show them,

'Here I'll show you,' he said, and Robin handed it to him; the man turned it on and began tuning it in.

'Listen,' he said, holding it close, they heard a voice say, *"Oscar, Victor, Lima, Tango"*.

'**WOW!**' said both Robin and Lucas in amazement.

'See,' he said.

'Let's see if we can get them to get those bullies,' said Robin.

'Don't be ridiculous,' said Lucas.

'Yeah, don't be a fool, *silly boy*! You can't speak back to them on this,' the man said. Even his Dog seemed to be laughing, or maybe he was just panting in the heat. The man switched off the radio and handed it back to Robin.

'What have you two been up to anyhow? Look at the state of you. You better not have been disturbing that badger set!'

'No,' said Lucas.

'Climbing trees then?'

'No,' said Robin.

'Well, what the devil have you been doing then?'

'We went to find some balls but got lynched by the bullies,' explained Robin.

'Well, that's one way to find some I suppose.'

Robin Laughed.

'Shut up Robin,' snapped Lucas.

The man tugged his Dog by the lead, 'Come on,' he said. leaving Robin and Lucas to carry on.

Once they'd got cleaned up, they decided to go to the phone box.

Lucas put ten pence into the coin slot when Robin realised Laura's number was at home.

'You idiot!' shouted Lucas. 'Go back and get it,' he said.

They were just coming back out of the phone box as Joan and Jane were getting off the Merry Hill minibus,

Joan asked,

'What were you two up to in that phone box?'

'Nothing,' said Robin.

'Yeah, right. You shouldn't play with the handset in those things, they're full of germs.'

'I feel sick,' said Robin looking very worried.

The four of them walked to Robin's house, Robin decided to call Laura from the home telephone instead,

'Hello?' said Laura.

'Hi,' said Robin.

'Oh, Hi Robin, I miss you.'

'I miss you too, I was going to phone you earlier from the phone box but there's too many germs.'

'What?' asked Laura.

'Why from a phone box?' She asked.

'Well, it was closer than coming home and Lucas had already put the money in.'

'But you're calling from the house phone? and Who's Lucas?'

Lucas pulled the handset from Robin's hand.

'Hi, I'm Lucas.'

'Hi, are you Robins' friend?'

'Yeah, has he told you about all the girls from school who fancy him?'

'No! He hasn't.'

'What are you doing?' asked Robin.

Lucas put his hand over the microphone,

'Shh, trust me,' he said.

'Well, he never stops talking about you, he turns all the other girls down because he's so fixed on you.'

'Well, I'm touched,' said Laura.

They went on talking, Lucas began to take the Mickey out of her accent, and she said he was cheeky and laughed.

Lucas gave the handset back to Robin.

'He's quite a comic isn't he your friend,' said Laura.

'Yeah, he's something,' said Robin.

'I don't like those other girls he was telling me about.'

'What other girls?' asked Robin.

Lucas slapped Robin on the arm and gave a frustrated look.

'Oh yeah, the girls, oh you don't need to worry about them, anyway, call me tomorrow, love you,' said Robin.

'Okay, I will. Bye, love you.'

Robin put down the phone.

'Why did you tell her other girls fancied me?' he asked.

'To keep her interested,' said Lucas.

'I don't have to do that, anyway, it's lying,' said Robin shamefully. 'I wish she was here though,' he added.

'Come on, let's go on a bike ride. That should cheer you up.'

'Okay, where shall we go?' asked Robin.

'How about we go down Himley and then cycle the South Staffs railway line?'

'I'll get my bike out of the garage,' said Robin.

'Great! Then we can go and get mine,' said Lucas.

Both Robin and Lucas went out the back to the garage, the garage was dark. The back window was mostly covered with overgrown clematis, and there were just a few beams of light shining through, illuminating the dusty air.

Robin pulled his bike from the wall,

'Look at how dusty this is,' he said.

He looked sad,

'I haven't ridden this since before I knew Laura.'

'Come on Robin cheer up, you can't think like that.'

'I can't help but think things like that,' said Robin.

'I don't know why you do this to yourself,' said Lucas looking at the bike.

Robin wheeled it out into the garden and through the veranda onto the drive.

They both walked to Lucas's to fetch his bike, Robin pushing his own. Lucas brought his bike out of his garage.

Chaucer Avenue was too steep to cycle, so they pushed until they reached Kiplin Road where it flattened out. They turned into Sandyfields Road and at the bend the entrance of Baggeridge Park.

They picked up their bikes and carried them over the gate.

They cycled the miner's path until they came to a marker post, it was about one and a half meters tall. Lucas stopped, and dismounted his bike,

'Hey check this out,' he said.

He ran up to it, grabbed the top with both hands and launched straight over the top.

Robin put his bike down and had a go.

Both began taking turns jumping the post.

'What the devil are you two doing now?' said the man with his dog, as he approached.

'We're jumping this stump,' said Robin.

'Well, I can see that. You know if your little game goes wrong, you won't be able to perform?'

'What do you mean?' asked Lucas.

'Come on lads give that a rest now.'

'Yeah, I've had enough anyway,' said Robin.

'Mr?' asked Robin.

'Call me Frank,' said the man. 'And what can I help you with?' he asked.

'Why do the police use Shakespeare?'

'What? They don't.'

'They do,' said Robin.

'I don't know what you mean boy,' said Frank.

'Well, all that talk, Romeo, Juliet.'

'*Yes?*' said Frank.

'You haven't been playing with that radio again, have you? He asked.

'*No*, well, what have the police got to do with Shakespeare?'

Frank looked confused.

'I reckon you've got your wires crossed there, they use the radiotelephonic alphabet,' he said.

'What's that?' asked Lucas.

'Well, to be frank, it's all the words they use like Alpha, Bravo,' explained Frank.

'But what's that got to do with Macbeth?' asked Robin.

Frank laughed,

'You're a funny one aren't you,' he said, 'Anyway, I must carry on walking Bernard. What are they teaching you in school these days?' he asked.

'Nothing,' said Robin.

'*Nothing*!' gasped Frank.

'Yeah, nothing, we've left school now,' said Robin.

Lucas nodded.

'Well shouldn't you both be looking for a job?' asked Frank.

'How can we, we're going up to secondary school after the holidays,' said Lucas.

Frank shook his head.

'Okay boys, be careful, and no more jumping over that post, all right.'

Frank pointed his finger at both Robin and Lucas and headed off.

They picked up their bikes and continued to Himley, they cycled passed Himley Hall and out the gates onto Himley Road. Continued to the disused railway walk and onto the canal in Hinksford.

They cycled for a short while when Robin had a fly go into his eye.

He bumped into Lucas and they both fell in.

A man steering his narrowboat laughed until he dropped his pint of honey ale in.

Robin and Lucas climbed out, Robin handed the pint glass back to the man, he snatched it and tipped out the water angrily. 'Let's go home', said Robin.

They cycled home soaking wet, and Lucas was in trouble with Lennard.

Robin managed to get his clothes washed, and on the line before anyone noticed, so he got away with it and was praised for doing his washing.

Brian gave him fifty pence, so Robin took it with Laura's details to the phone box.

He called her and her dad answered, and asked if Robin could wait so she could call him back in five

175

minutes, Robin asked if she could dial 1,4,7,1, and press 3, as he was calling from a phone box.

Robin sat on the curb outside the phone box and waited until the phone started to ring. It was Laura, she said how much she was missing him and asked if he would be going to the caravan park next year.

'I'm not sure,' he said. 'I want to but I'm sure my family will most likely want to go back to blooming Bournemouth again.'

'Oh, that's a shame, I was hoping to see you again,' said Laura.

'Me too,' said Robin frustratedly.

Then Robin came up with an idea,

'Tell you what,' he said.

'What?' asked Laura.

'Let's agree on a time later,'

'Yes,' said Laura excitedly.

'Shall we say six o'clock tonight?'

'Yes, okay,' she said.

'Well, you know how all the roads in this country are connected?'

'I suppose so,' said Laura wondering where Robin was going with this.

'Well, if you touch the road outside yours with your palm and I do the same, it will be like we are touching hands, won't it? since all the roads may as well be the same piece of tarmac.'

'I don't think they are, but it's a romantic gesture,' said Laura.

'Will you, do it?' asked Robin.

'Sure,' said Laura.

That night Robin did exactly that, he left the front door on the latch, walked to the road and knelt at the kerb's edge.

The (541) bus service came down the road and blasted its horn at Robin, he jumped back with a scare.

He decided to try around the corner of Wordsworth Road.

Frank and his dog walked by,

'What the devil are you up to this time?' he asked.

Robin explained he was trying to touch hands with Laura.

Frank asked if Robin was okay and if he'd had a bump to the head from jumping the marker post.

'No? Hey Frank.'

'Yes?'

'Do you have the time?'

'Why, it's half past six.'

'Oh, good. I can get back in time for

"Round the Twist".

'I should say it's too late for that my boy.' Said Frank.

August 21ˢᵗ, 1997

Lucas called for Robin; he was late because he'd been watching *"Bay watch"*.

They decided to go down to the Green. They were near Longfellow and Shakespeare School as music could be heard distinctly from the direction of the assembly hall.

'Is that music I can hear?' asked Robin.

'Yeah, it's coming from the school,' said Lucas.

'Let's get closer and listen,' Lucas suggested.

They both walked into the open gates of the school grounds. Mrs Singer was seen playing her guitar through the great doors and singing "The Skye Boat Song". Robin felt a twinge of nostalgia as the familiar sound of guitar and her voice was heard.

They found Mr Bourneview on the playing field as they walked the perimeter of the grounds. He was poking a long stick up into a tree, and they walked over to him.

'What are you doing sir?' asked Lucas.

'I'm trying to get rid of this wasp nest.'

'Is that dangerous sir?' Asked Robin.

'Nah, it's fine,' replied Mr Bourneview.

Mr Bourneview jumped up and pierced the stick straight through the paper nest. Immediately the wasps shot out fiercely and gave chase.

'Run for your lives!' screamed Mr Bourneview.

'*Ahh*! What have you done!' shouted Lucas.

'Oh, Knickers!' Blurted Robin.

They ran as fast as they could screaming towards the kid's nursery.

'Let us in!' cried Mr Bourneview.

'No!' said a nursery assistant.

'Please, we're gonna die,' screeched Lucas.

'What do you mean you're going to, Oh My! Get in quick.'

The wasps began to come in through the broken window.

'Ahh! Have you not fixed that yet?' yelped Mr Bourneview.

'Obviously not,' said Lucas.

Mr Bourneview picked up a fire extinguisher and went to throw it at the fierce wasps.

'No! Don't do that,' said the nursery assistant.

'You'll make them savage,' said Lucas.

'They're already savage,' said Mr Bourneview.

Robin grabbed it from him and blasted carbon dioxide towards the hole.

Another nursery assistant, (Natalie) climbed a chair and blocked the hole with a kiddie's chalkboard.

'Oi! Stop looking at my bum you.'

'I wasn't,' said Lucas.

'You were_'

'Shut up Robin!' snapped Lucas.

'Why were those wasps so angry?' asked Natalie,

Robin pointed at Mr Bourneview.

'He poked their nest with a stick,' said Lucas.

'Why am I not surprised? Have you not got a caretaker?' she asked.

'No, he walked out a month ago,' said Mr Bourneview disappointedly.

'You ain't right you ain't,' said Natalie.

'Better stay here a while, that's a proper savage swarm out there,' said Mr Bourneview.

August 22nd, 1997

Robin called for Lucas, and they both decided to walk to Gornal to meet Joan after finishing her cleaning round.

There was a huge crowd gathered outside Roberts Hill Primary opposite.

'What's going on?' asked Lucas.

'I'm not sure,' said Robin.

'I don't believe it,' said Lucas.

'What?' asked Robin.

'Look, it's Sir Griff Prichard,' said Lucas.

'Never!' said Robin.

'It is, look,' said Lucas.

'Flip me! It is,' said Robin.

'What's he doing here?' asked Robin.

There was a ribbon tied to the school gate on one end and wrapped around the oak tree on the other.

Sir Griff cut it, and everyone cheered.

Joan came out of the house she had finished cleaning and just in time not to miss the event and found Robin and Lucas.

'What is he doing Mom?' asked Robin.

'He's declaring the school open,' said Joan. 'I told you about this weeks ago. You never listen, do you?

A nice man called David came over and greeted Joan. She introduced him to Robin and David shook Robin by the hand. David gave Robin a vinyl record which was "Dave Pope and John Daniels Love Offering".

It was signed *"To Rupert, peace be with you."*

'Thank you, Sir,' said Robin.

'You're very welcome son,' he said.

Sir Griff began to sing a song on the inflatable stage, that was, *"We Don't Talk Anymore"* by Cliff Richard.

August 23rd, 1997

Robin walked down to Himley Hall and onto Wall Heath. He walked by Kate's Crusty Crusts and saw Roy Jones; a friend of Jack sitting inside at a table. Robin went inside, 'Oh hello Robin, said Roy, as he placed his cup of tea down on the table. 'Would you like an iced bun?' he offered as he reached into a carrier bag.

'A nice bun,' asked Robin.

'No, an iced bun,' said Roy, 'but yes they are nice.' He added.

'Eh, herm!' said Kate sharply. 'The only bun, bap, or roll he'll be having is one of mine! *Thank you very much.*'

Roy looked meekly at Robin. 'Cup of tea? He asked. Roy pulled twenty pence from his trouser pocket, 'Here Kate, a cup for Robin as well, please. Kate walked over and took the twenty pence out of his hand in a stern manner.

Roy offered his bag of goodies to Robin. 'A lovely raisin biscuit?'

'Don't even think about it you!' Kate said sharply. 'And will you please stop propping your bike up against my shop window? You still owe me from when your ladder went through the last one.'

'Yes, but I've cleaned the new one for free since.'

'Yes, well just keep your bag of treats to yourself and stop giving them to all my customers'.

Kate brought Robin's tea over. Robin's face turned sour when he tasted it.

'Right! That's it you two get out!' she snapped abruptly. 'If you want proper tea bugger off to John Sparry next door and take that pantry of a bag and that blooming bike with you.

'What a splendid idea,' said Roy. 'Mr Sparry is always very hospitable and would always offer a cracking cup of tea upon a visit, which is if he's not too busy.'

'Sounds like a good place to go when you feel down as I do,' said Robin.

'Go on then! Before I drag you both there myself,' said Kate beginning to wipe over the table, nudging Roy's arm off the edge.

Robin and Roy got up and left. They walked next door to Mr Sparry's Book and Antique shop. Robin followed Roy inside and was astonished by the large number of books that were in there. Roy disappeared into the back and Robin was left open-mouthed staring at all the books.

'Now that's what I call a cup of tea!' Robin heard Roy speak from the back room beyond the draped curtain dividing both rooms.

Once refreshed with traditionally made tea, both Robin and Roy left Mr Sparry's house as Roy checked his watch.

'I better get round and clean Mrs Payne's window,' he said mounting his bike. 'Come with me Robin, she makes a lovely cup of tea.'

Robin followed as Roy nearly took a passing car's side window out with his ladder balanced on his bike.

Steadily Roy cycled at a walking pace with the ladder, bag of snacks and bucket hanging from the handlebars.

It wasn't far until they reached Mrs Payne's house and Roy began to fill up his bucket from the garden tap.

'Hello Roy,' said Mrs Payne as she appeared from the top window. 'Would you and your friend like a cup of tea?'

'Oh, yes please Mrs Payne,' said Roy.

'*Oh*, not for me thanks,' said Robin, not being able to stomach any more.

'Here comes Mr Thatcher,' said Roy. 'Over here.'

Roy waved and encouraged Mr Thatcher to come and join him and Robin in the front garden.

Mr Thatcher came over and leaned on his walking stick.

'Hello Mr Thatcher,' said Robin.

'Well hello Robert,' said Mr Thatcher. 'Fancy seeing you in here.'

'I'm not Robert, I'm Robin,' said Robin.

'Oh, I'm sorry Please forgive me, Rupert,' said Mr Thatcher.

'Never mind,' said Robin.

Roy began to show off his windup radio and it began to rain heavily. Mrs Payne rushed outside, 'Come on inside Gentlemen, you'll get soaked through.

The fire was lit in the kitchen with a kettle placed into it heating up.

It was an old house complete with a stoneware sink. The kettle began to boil, and Mrs Payne pulled it out from the fire using a tea towel.

'Ah, here we are,' she said pouring the tea into four cups.

'How long you had this place?' asked Mr Thatcher.

'Oh, I've lived here all my life, it was once my Grandparents and as you can see, I've worked hard to keep it in the same condition, by not doing anything to it at all,' replied Mr Payne.

'Well, I must say, I'm impressed,' said Mr Thatcher.

'Thank you, you won't find a house like this nowadays, not unless you visit the Black Country Museum or John Sparry's antiques in Town.'

'Yes,' said Mr Thatcher that's where The Crooked House has gone.'

'Don't be ridiculous,' said Mr Payne, 'I was only in there earlier.'

'You mean The Crooked House is in John Sparry's house?' asked Robin curiously.

'Don't be foolish silly boy! said Mr Payne. The Crooked House hasn't moved.

'Well, if the Crooked House hasn't moved, where had I gone?' asked Mr Thatcher. 'That was a lovely cup of tea by the way,' he added.

'The stupid kids have smashed the bus shelter again,' said Mr Payne as he gazed out the window.

'Have they!' boomed Mr Thatcher. 'They need to bring corporal punishment back,' he said in anger.

And at that, Mr Thatcher launched his cup into the fire.

It smashed with a blast causing Mr Payne to jolt and Roy to drop his.

'I'll see myself out,' said Mr Thatcher as he closed the door behind him.

'What's his problem?' asked Mr Payne.

My uncle Jack thinks the war turned his mind,' said Robin.

'I think your uncle's right,' replied Mr Payne. 'Who is he again?' he asked.

'Mr Thatcher,' said Roy.

'Mr Thatcher ay? Hmm, Mr Thatcher the teacup smasher more like,' said Mr Payne.

That evening Robin fell asleep on his bed, he'd been reading about the Boeing 727 aeroplane from a book John Sparry had sold him.

He lay there, his eyes flickered as he dreamed with the collapsed book resting on his chest. 'where's the engine?' he asked as he spoke in his sleep.

He was a castaway on a small island and had found an abandoned jet aeroplane which was missing one of its engines, 'If I can find the engine I can get home,' he wondered. He searched the island and found it stranded on the beach. Rolling it along the ground he got it to the deserted airplane. He built a

193

platform under the wing using broken caravan parts. Robin pulled the engine up onto the platform and attached it back onto the aeroplane. He climbed the wing and got in through the emergency door, walked down to the cockpit and Jack was waiting for him in the co-pilot seat. Robin saw they were sitting on a huge runway and no longer in a jungle. There was a key left in the ignition and Robin turned it. There was a roar as the jet engines fired up. Robin disengaged the parking brake and pushed the engine thrust throttle levers to the position, TO/GA, "Take off/Go around". Robin and Jack were pushed back into their seats hard. 'Don't do that! Said Jack. 'You'll blow our bloody heads off! He continued, 'There's only us on here, you only need that much power in an emergency or when fully loaded.'

Jack pulled the levers to the climb position and the engines rolled back to a steady state. The aeroplane climbed up high. The engines rolled back to idle! There was an audible warning sounding and a warning light flashing. It was the fuel level warning and the engines cut out completely. There was a silence as the power also failed. Jack looked at Robin, 'That's done it' he said. 'You didn't check the fuel before we left did you!' He left his seat and grabbed a parachute from beneath. He parachuted out of the emergency door and Robin was left at the controls. The only sound that was left was the sound of rushing air as it rushed through the wings. The aeroplane lost momentum falling towards the ground Robin was pushed back to the seat, the g-force was terrific. Bang! Robin awoke hitting his head on the bedroom floor.

Chapter 10
SORROW THE LIBRARY AND THE SWAMP

Robin was sitting in the library; he hadn't heard from Laura for quite some time.

He was daydreaming while gazing down the long valley of books. It's so quiet in there, it's dull outside but muggy with a gentle breeze coming in through the window.

He got up and found *"The Secret Diary of Adrian Mole age thirteen and three-quarters,"* and put it back.

He just couldn't face reading the same book he knew Laura was reading.

'Just think, I'll be reading that book and all the time wondering where Laura has got to or what she thought or even if she's finished it at all.'

He picked up another book from the non-fiction section, it was called *"The Great Flood Of 1953- flood disaster in East Anglia and Essex"*.

'Why did they not teach us this at school,' said Robin aloud, turning the pages.

'**Shh**!' a strict Librarian said sharply.

He turned back to the book, 'This is worth borrowing,' he thought.

His mind went back to thinking about Laura and how much he missed her. Over and over, he began to replay the memories in his head, but that only

made him more lovesick.

There were no words to explain what he was going through; he could only compare these feelings to when you get goosebumps from listening to a certain song but oppositely and negatively.

Remembering the excitement, he had in his life had vanished, and along with the absence of sunshine, he just wished to re-live the whole event again, rather than trying to re-live the memory.

He dried his eyes with the back of his hand and got up out of his chair again.

He went over to the window and saw others outside walking by.

Some lads about his age were laughing amongst themselves, Robin felt distant from the rest of the world and wondered if Laura was going through the same, or if she was just getting on with her life.

Then his uncle Jack walked in, he saw that Robin was alone and went over to him.

Robin told Jack everything that had happened in the last few weeks.

Jack smiled and rested his hand on Robin's shoulder.

'It's better to have loved than not at all,' he said.

'I'm not so sure, only a few days of pure happiness for a lifetime of pain.'

'No, that can't be true,' said Jack. 'Makes you feel alive though, doesn't it?'

'Maybe, but I don't want to feel this pain anymore.'

'No of course you don't, but you wouldn't be human if you didn't feel it would you.'

'When do you think it will go away?'

'Maybe, never,' said Jack.

Robin called for Lucas the next day.

They walked to Cotwallend Valley, and Lucas took his football with them. They had walked some distance, probably half a mile along the old coach road.

'Did you know Lori and Rich are courting now?' Lucas asked as he examined his football while carrying it.

'No,' said Robin, 'What does courting mean?'

'Oh no, not this again,' said Lucas.

'You mean going out?' asked Robin.

'Yes Robin, going out,' said Lucas.

'I'm not interested, I'm missing Laura,' said Robin glumly.

'Hey, Kate's been asking about you.'

'So?' said Robin.

Lucas was bouncing his football on the ground as they walked.

Suddenly he lost control of it, and it left the path, rolled off the edge and down a steep embankment.

'Oh no!' Lucas cried.

Both Robin and Lucas peered down.

'There it is,' said Robin, 'How are we supposed to get down there?'

'Over there, look there's a few rocks we can climb,' said Lucas.

They walked further along the path until they came to the rocks which were embedded in the cliff edge. They took their time, carefully climbing down. Eventually, they reached the bottom. Lucas pointed 'Look it's on that grass,' he said.

The football was sat on what seemed to be immaculate and lush green grass.

'Let's have a kickabout here on this grass for a bit,' he suggested.

Lucas ran towards the ball and Robin followed, they ran and with a massive splash disappeared into the green slimy lake.

As they came back up to the surface, they were covered in muddy water.

'Ergh! "It's a swamp," expressed Lucas disgustedly.

'It's like the swamp in "The Neverending Story", said Robin.

"The Neverending Story" by Michael Ende 1979. Translated by Ralph Manheim, 1983. Film adaptation by Warner Bros, 1984?'

'Yes, that's the one.'

'We've got to get out of here,' said Lucas.

They struggled to climb out as there was nothing to grab onto, and the soft edge only came in as they tried to pull themselves out.

'Can you touch the bottom?' asked Robin.

'No,' cried Lucas.

In a panic, they began to shout for help, but they were so deep in the valley that nobody would hear them.

In their panic, the turbulence they made caused the weakest point of the swamp to burst its banks. All the water began to flow into the stream far below.

The ball went first, then Robin and Lucas got flushed away with it. They were carried downstream until the large body of water had drained, leaving them lying on the stream's stony bed. They were both out of breath, Lucas was on his back and said, 'That's my ball gone then.'

Robin felt sad for Lucas as he remembered the two of them playing football together with it, on the school playground, which they would never return. They got up out of the stream and went home.

Robin walked home after waving goodbye to Lucas as he was carried in by Lennard, so as not to get the carpet wet. Robin explained to Brien that he and Lucas had lost Lucas's football in the stream in Cotwallend, and asked where Lucas's football might be by now. 'Probably the River Severn at Stourport,' replied Brien watching TV. Once showered and dried, Robin sat in front of the television and an advert for a new Volvo came on. "The Windmills of Your Mind" by Noel Harrison, was the song that was used. This caused Robin to sweat with great sadness as it reminded him of the day, he was alone in Norfolk, staring at the surreal windmill that time had forgotten.

Joan was concerned about him since he didn't seem like his usual self anymore.

All he wanted to do was lay on his back on his bed and stare at the ceiling. She knew the reason and asked if he was missing Laura and if he wanted to talk about it. He said missing Laura was hurting so bad, and he was sad about losing Lucas's Wolves football too.

Robins' mom explained that he was pining for Laura and that it was all normal to feel that way.

'Pity people who don't have such feelings,' she said.

'But I want it to stop, and I can't.'

'I know Bob, she must be feeling the same way as you are too.'

'Do you think so?' he asked.

'Yes, I saw the way she looked at you enough times. And anyway, she was the one who made the first move wasn't she?'

'Yeah, I suppose,' sighed Robin.

'Well then, and she did look very sad when you both exchanged your details. Here, I'll make you a nice calming cup of lavender tea.'

'I wasn't sad at the time, I thought I was going to see her again. This is unbearable! You're given someone who likes you, and then they get snatched away back out of your life just like that. It's such a sad situation.'

'That's life, I suppose,' sighed Joan. 'Those bullies who like to fight harmless boys and cause trouble, they are the ones who truly miss out,' she said.

Robin was confused, 'Miss out?' he asked.

'Yes, what do you think they were up to when you were romancing with Laura? Spending time with smart girls? No! They were just most likely being stupid and up to no good as usual, smashing up phone boxes and bus shelters. A sponge to society they are!

If you're going to have pity, pity them. They are the ones in a real sad situation.'

Robin retired into the back garden. He settled on the lawn at the bottom close to the silver birch. He watched the leaves as they danced in the breeze.

All he could think about was Laura and the desire to share the moment with her. Listening to the leaves in the warm breeze imitated to sound of the sea. Robin was immersed in a sense of loneliness and decided to go out for a walk alone. He walked up the road and passed the golf course he loved so much.

He continued and walked through an alley which led him through the Brownswall estate.

The wind blew him back taking his breath, dust blew up in his eyes and the smell of creosote from the sun-baked fence panels got up his nose.

He crossed the road and followed another alley which brought him to a vast field, there was no other person there, only himself.

There was an old 1970s-type slide in the middle, and he sat at the bottom of it.

Lucas was out with Lauren because she had come back home from her holiday.

Robin was thinking that he wouldn't spend much time with Lucas anymore since they both were starting different schools in September.

He sat there for a while just daydreaming when a small Jack Russel skipped by.

Robin looked around wondering if the dog was lost, and then a young lady appeared from the alley to the field and called.

'There you are!' She said carrying his lead.

He came up to Robin and licked his hand.

'Come on you,' she said, as she walked over.

She picked the little dog up and smiled at Robin.

'Sorry about that,' she said.

 'What's his name?' Robin asked.

'Jack.' She replied.

'Proper name,' said Robin.

She smiled again, 'Thanks.' She put Jack back on the ground and walked away. Robin watched her and Jack walk into the distance until he could see them no longer, and decided it was a good time to go home.

Chapter 11

REVISITATION

Twenty years had passed, and Robin had booked a caravan holiday online a week ago. He is packing a suitcase at the last minute and is having a few missed words with himself from struggling to fit everything in. 'Why won't you just piggin fit!'

Eventually remembering where he had put his electric shaver, he finally got everything in his car. He drove to Himley Road petrol station to fill up for the journey. Once he arrived, he stepped out of the car, removed the petrol nozzle and began to fill up. Suddenly the manager came rushing out.

'Should you be putting petrol in that mate?' he asked as he shouted from across the forecourt.

'Uh?' muttered Robin. 'I've always put petrol in it,' he said.

The manager came over to him and had a closer look at the car.

'Are you sure you don't put diesel in this?'

'Yes!' said Robin.

'Sorry I could have sworn this was a diesel, but now I see it's an 'M' reg S40 Volvo, you don't see many of these around these days.'

'No, I guess not,' said Robin, 'But I love it.'

'Well, my friend, when you're done come and ask about my new Black Country fizzy aid promo, I've got going on inside.

Robin wondered.

'Black country fizzy aid ay? What flavour is it?'

'Toffee Offal,' replied the manager. "Goes down well with pork scratchings".

He shook Robin by the hand and went back inside.

'I'd rather have a pack of salty beef balls,' thought Robin. "Ugh, *toffee Offal*".

After Robin had fuelled the car, he paid without giving any attention to the Toffee Offal promotion stand, got back to his car and drove away heading for the M6 motorway.

'Maybe toffee offal was meant to be toffee Opple,' thought Robin, "was it a misprint?" he wondered.

"Opple translates from Black Country dialect to Apple in English".

Robin began his journey, he passed through the City of Leicester and on the Radio, *"The Drugs Don't Work"* by The Verve was playing as he passed by the towering tower blocks of the 1960s.

It had been some time on the road and Robin needed a break. He Pulled off the A47 and found an old pub called "The Coach, The Horse, and The Highwayman Inn". It sounded more inviting than "The Lion, The Witch, and the Cradle Snatcher," across the road, so Robin parked the car in the car park of The Coach, The Horse, and The Highwayman Inn and went inside for some refreshment. He bought a pint of dandelion and burdock since he was driving. He also ordered a bowl of chips with a cheese and ham toastie. Others had stopped off as they were on their way to a holiday of their own and were also enjoying refreshments inside the pub. A popular music channel was on a large TV which was situated on the wall behind the bar.

As it happened, Sinead O'Conner's *"Nothing Compares 2 U,"* was playing, and Robin began to look back upon his life. "*Holding Back the Years"* by Simply Red was up next, Robin got himself together and was ready for the next leg of his journey, so he headed back to the old Volvo.

He drove along Queen Elizabeth II Way and eventually, he passed through Snettisham. He began to get the seaside vibe from driving along the sandy twisty lanes as he reached the resort where he would be staying for the week.

Finally, he checked in at reception and found his caravan.

He unpacked his belongings and after setting up his smart speaker, he sat at the dining table, opened a can of Captain of the Morning and listened to *"Born Slippy"* by Underworld (1997). He felt his stubble and found his electric shaver but realised he'd forgotten the charger as the shaver's battery ran out. He felt his stubble once more and looked into the bathroom mirror, 'Stop growing all the time you git!' He said. He put on his green duffle coat and headed to the beach.

He noticed the beach bar had long gone since his last visit. He listened to the waves for a short while before walking on.

He strolled back to the site, feeling a thirst for a refreshing drink. As he entered the clubhouse, his eyes lit up at the sight of "Suffolk punch" on tap, a local speciality he had always longed to try. A friendly and cheerful staff member greeted him warmly, he asked for a well-deserved "Suffolk Punch" and so she poured him a generous pint.

'Have you come far?' she asked.

'Yes, I've come from Stourbridge,' he replied paying contactless for the drink with his card.

'I haven't heard of Stourbridge before,' she said. 'How long has that taken you?

'About four hours, It's between Worcester and Wolverhampton.'

'Oh, Birmingham, right?'

'No, "not quite."

'Well, you sound like a Brummie to me.'

'Thanks a bunch,' said Robin with a chuckle.

'Well, I hope you have a nice stay here at Heacham,' and handed the freshly poured pint over to him.

'Thanks,' he said taking a sip.

Robin explained that the last time he was in Heacham was the summer of 1997. 'Oh wow,' she said. 'I bet a lot has changed here since then.'

'Yes, much has,' said Robin taking another sip bigger than the first.

The nice lady stared in astonishment as Robin gulped the apple pulp.

'Here, "see this coin?" He said after pulling it from his coat pocket.

'Yes.'

'My Uncle Dave gave it to me all those years ago the last time I was here, I thought I'd spent it, but I must have got it mixed up with another two-pound coin I already had in my pocket at the time. I've kept it ever since,' Robin held it in the palm of his hand. 'Here take it, have it as a tip,' he said.

'But you've had that all this time, I can't possibly take it from you now, it must be sentimental to you?'

'Hey, don't worry about it, I've been holding onto the past for far too long,' he said as he held it up to the light while turning it in his fingers.

He put it back and smiled, 'At least I have my memories,' he said. 'I'll see you around.'

'You sure will,' she said and attended another guest.

Taking his pint of "Suffolk punch" outdoors, Robin occupied a bench on the Bar terrace. He saw a large old shed with one of the double doors ajar, which was over by the laundrette. He walked over to it with his pint. Inside was an old worn pool table covered in dust and cobwebs. He noticed it in the dark and moved inside to get a better look. He didn't realise it was the one he and Laura had played with together all those years ago until he noticed the acid house smiley that was still on it that Daniel had stuck on. He moved back to the bar terrace and overheard music playing out from the outdoor speakers of the Bar terrace, which was *"Lifelines"* by a-ha.

In

Loving Memory of

Jack Wall

1917-2004

In

Loving Memory of

Roy Jones

1942-2023

A c k n o w l e d g e m e n t

Other books and well-known songs that are in this story have been respectfully mentioned for the sole purpose of appreciation and remembrance of their existence, especially the stories by other Authors for the joy they can bring in the current read declining climate we are sadly facing.

The television programme "**Knightmare**" is a game show created by Tim Child which was broadcast on CITV from 7 September 1987 to 11 November 1994 by Anglia Television. The television programme, Crystal Craze is a spoof of "**The Crystal Maze**" which aired on channel 4 from 1990 to 1995. It returned in 2016 and three more series followed from 2017 to 2020.

"Round the Twist" is an Australian children's comedy-drama television series which ran from 1989 to 2001.

Just to let you know The Armageddon stratagem does not exist and is completely fictional so don't go out searching for it. All artwork was generated by Microsoft Bing/ DALL-E artificial intelligence assistant.

Special Thanks

Thank you to Local Historian "John Sparry", for permitting me to mention you and shop in my story. Dear Friends, please give John Sparry and his old Book and Antique shop a visit or visit online; (johnsparry.co.uk).

Thanks to Lori Boswell for having patience with me while writing this book.

Through the rippled glass of the door, I peer into the past, captivated by the winter sun as it filters through. The colours outside, softened and muted, distort reality, making it seem as if the past is within arm's reach. Out there, beyond the door, lies the place where we danced to upbeat music, where life pulsed with vitality. In here, the present intrudes a humble fire crackling, its warmth mingling with the laughter of the unaware. By the open fire, seated on a stool with a beer in hand, I find solace. Yet, sometimes, when the newcomer steps through the door, the bitter cold rushes in. It's then that I ponder: Could this winter sun be the same summer sun we once played under, long ago?

At the bottom of a **grassy bank** stands an old oak tree.

Two hundred or more summers it has seen.
All those people that have been running around, here there
not moving an inch.

How many times has the grass been cut? Did you see it
grow?
How many leaves have been shed?
How many times has the tide gone out?

Spring to Summer,
Winter to Spring,

Have you kept count of the times it rained?
Have you remembered every lightning strike?
Have you come close?

When did the acorn grow?
When did it all start?
Where are we going?
What are we doing?

Whatever happened when you walked that beach?
Wasn't it nice?

What happened when she saw you for the first
time? Didn't it feel good?

Whatever happened when time didn't wait?
Wasn't it fast?

What Happened when she climbed the fence to see you?
Didn't you peer over but were too late?

Whatever happened when the music
stopped when the rain came? Wasn't it mad?

Whatever happened when you won her heart?
What about when she broke yours?

Whatever happened when the dream was over?
Wasn't it sad?

Feel that breeze, hear that sail,
Smell that grass, see that hail.
Drink your tea, eat your chips,
Catch some fish and fake that smile.
Run that hill, take your time,
Walk the beach and learn that line.
Touch that wall, watch that sea,
Stand up tall and unlock that door.

Happisburgh
There once lay a field not far away,
Also, a church across the way.
The lighthouse the pub,
The cattle the shrub,
Even the people did all that they could.
In came the tide and took out the side,
Now all that can be said is bye and goodbye.

Play your record,
Swing on the swing,
Play the recorder,
The fun has begun.

Run about yelling,
Share all that is there.
Swim around telling
and
Find someone to
care!

Explore everything,
With no time to spare
And do not despair,
When all seems
unfair.

Somewhere nice somewhere new,
The sky is blue but where are you?
The Sun is bright and when it set it was quite the sight.
The piano still plays, the song goes on,
But how do I continue?
The Sun still shines, the wind still blows,
The waves still crash, an empty hall,
A lonely beach, and you're still out of reach.

One Summer
You'll find me in the field,

You'll find me on the lake.

You'll find me in the rain.

You'll hear me on the stage,

You'll see me in the cage.

Play your songs and

You'll find me by your side.

Take it   **easy!**
Take your guitar down to the Green,

Play it and sing,

Watch them gather,

See them come,

See the air take your hair.

Let's take lemonade,

Let's take it easy.

The Fall

225

When the leaves have all fallen,
When all the summertime has run out,
Will you remember?

When the cold and dark cometh forthwith,
Will you forget?

In the night, the cold foggy night, will you hear?

When the chill closes in and the smell of burnt coal passes
by your house,
Will you still be mine?

The Walk home in the cool rain was dull,
After the band had played
their cheerful songs.
The leaves are falling,
and the clouds are dark.
The brook has burst its banks,
and the land has begun to slide.
The old path has collapsed into the valley,
It's a long and far way round.
It's miserable, cold and nobody around.

The Knights Quest

On those dark winter nights return home swiftly.

Return with your sword of truth,

Never surrender when they try and capture your land,

And hold on to your faith.

Keep on your armour, the shield of hope.

The fire is a flame, and the stew is still warm inside.

Hold on to your shield when the icy blast closes in.

The banquet with be ready and waiting,

On your return when your quest is over.

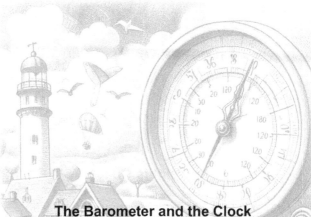

The Barometer and the Clock
The blossom has only just bloomed,
And the Sun has begun to rise.
So, let us go back; Back to the place where it all began.
Where time was long, and the summer was fun.
Let go our troubles,
and leave behind our fears.

The scent of nature's perfume takes its usual grip on me.
Qué hermoso día,
What a beautiful day reads the Barometer.

Alas, hurry now.
The Clock has been ticking long now and soon the
Barometer might also agree.
Let us run then.

Let us run outdoors, before the winter Taketh away the
chance to hear the music and the smell of this sweet
perfume of Summer.

Before the Barometer catches the clock let us fly.
Be wise my friends watch Barometer and also listen to
The Clock.

In the 90's

They were the best of friends,
They shared their dreams and secrets,
Unknowingly there was no end.

They played their games and music,
They rode their bikes and fished.
They explored the whole of the Straits,
They had so much to be grateful for.

They grew up in a time of change,
As analogue was becoming obsolete.

COMING SOON!

Printed in Great Britain
by Amazon

39675415R00131